THE TURNED

LAST OF THE GARGOYLES BOOK 2

FoxTales Press

DANI HOOTS

The Turned
Last of the Gargoyles, #2
© 2021 Dani Hoots
Content Edits by Justin Boyer
Cover Design Copyright © 2021 by Biserka Designs
Formatting by Dani Hoots
All rights reserved.

ISBN for paperback: 978-1-942023-83-8

ISBN for hardcover: 978-1-942023-84-5

CHAPTER ONE

Gwen

Flashing lights filled Gwen's sight, almost blinding her. Why clubs used lights like this was beyond Gwen. She missed the old-style pubs or even the old pagan rituals when everyone drank some secret drink and suddenly it was three days later, and everyone was naked and passed out in a field. Those were the good ol' days.

The music was rather loud, hurting the generals' rather sensitive ears. All twelve generals had acute hearing—they were predators after all. The minions they had created also had improved hearing, but not quite as strong. The air was filled with sweat, pheromones, and alcohol. Soon it would smell of blood.

Gwen took another deep breath. Yes, so much fresh blood for the taking, but she knew she couldn't indulge. This was a mission to create minions, not to create chaos. She sighed. The latter was always more fun though, but she wasn't in charge. No, she lost that privilege long ago. No one trusted her now, so she would have to follow as close as she could to their rules, which would be quite a task for her. She never liked following rules.

Gwen felt James's arm wrap around her the two of them and Jürgen and Seth approached the bouncer at the club. The bouncer was tall, at least six feet, had cannon-sized arms and tree trunks for legs. His body was covered in tattoos from his neck down to his legs, ranging from skulls to dark symbols and words of death and destruction. He would have been intimidating if she weren't a demon and the fact that he was already a minion. They had turned him earlier in the week so they could gain access to the club, and once they were inside, the bouncer wouldn't let another soul in. Or out.

As they approached, the bouncer grinned, revealing a gold-capped tooth. He opened the door, and they all stepped inside. The door locked behind them, and everything was set.

Techno music filled Gwen's ears. She couldn't help but smile and tap her foot along with it. Germany brought back so many memories—memories she'd thought she would never enjoy again.

She had been a fool to think she could repent for her wrongdoings. There was no repenting for her—there was no going back. No matter what she did, she would never be forgiven or let back into Heaven, so why even bother? James had made her come to that realization, and she loved him for it. He would never let her go, no matter what she did. She didn't deserve him, and she knew it. They had left Heaven to be with each other. Neither of them desired power but the ability to love. Love wasn't allowed in Heaven, at least not the love that they wanted. Lucifer promised them they could be together as long as they did what he asked.

That was centuries ago. Why had she suddenly felt bad for all her wrongdoings? A demon can't live and have a guilty conscience. All she could do now was live on Earth or suffer in hell. Lucky for her, Earth was for the taking. All they had to do was finish off the Gargoyles and Lucifer would be released and finally have reign over these lands.

"These humans don't have a care in the world, do they?" Gwen laughed as she examined the people dancing around her. Most of the humans were what they considered dancing closely. It was more like grinding and, well, having sex on the dance floor. Germany was a lot more lax on sex clubs, and that was apparent in front of them.

"They never do." James kissed her hand.

Gwen closed her eyes as his hot lips touched her skin. As her eyes opened, they flashed yellow. Her hunger was deep, and she could drink the blood of every person in the club. If she wasn't careful, she just might. The night was still young, and she wanted to have her fill. Hopefully she could get some blood after this. Gwen glanced at James's neck. Perhaps just her blood-bonded partner would be enough.

"Will you two knock it off?" Jürgen growled. "We are here to get minions, not alert everyone and cause chaos."

"But Jürgen, where's the fun in that?" She spun around, taking in all the pleasure surrounding her. "Chaos is so much more satisfying."

"And if you hadn't betrayed us like you did, then we

would be able to enjoy chaos, so get over it. We are on a mission." He glared at her. He always did that, even before she betrayed them. He was still mad at her for something that had happened between the two of them centuries before. Since he wouldn't forgive her, she liked making his life a living hell. And he knew that.

Gwen just grinned. "So demanding. All right, we'll do it your way. Who wants to check the emergency exits?"

Darrell raised his hand. "I will! I will!" In an instant he disappeared and reappeared. "Done and done."

Gwen chuckled as she looked at Darrell. She was happy to be working with him again as he made missions all the more entertaining for various reasons. He always got the job done, and he was humorous about it. He was as playful as she was, but they had a more brother-sister type relationship. He went with her crazy ideas, ones that even lasted centuries. She had missed him over the past eighty years, especially his fear of drums. Why he was afraid, she still wasn't sure. It all happened centuries before, after he had gotten back from America. He never told a soul what happened, and the demon that was there was destroyed by one of the Gargoyles.

She raised her arms in the air. "Then let us turn these bodies into vessels and bring forth our brethren!"

None of the humans around them seemed to notice Gwen's declaration but kept on partying. There were five of them and hundreds of humans, but that didn't matter. It would be merely minutes before all of them were bitten and killed—transforming them all into minions.

Gwen grabbed the closest human and sank her fangs into the woman's throat. She was probably in her early twenties, just there to have a good time. The man she had been dancing with didn't even try to stop Gwen but turned to run. James was on him in seconds, his blood soon gushing out on the dance floor.

It took a while for the entire club to realize what was happening, but when they did, they all ran for the door. Screams echoed across the dance floor as more and more bodies hit the ground. Everything was stained red, Gwen's favorite color.

The DJ kept the music going, ignoring everything that happened around him. They'd made sure they turned him the night before. They didn't want the music to stop—where would be the fun in that? Gwen loved a soundtrack in the background. It made it that much better.

Gwen took a deep breath—the scent of fear and blood filling her nostrils. Blood also covered her lips and hands, with splatters across her clothes. She glanced around to find her fellow generals also taking in the pleasures of the chaos. She wished she could let some get away so that more chaos would resonate though the city, but they couldn't yet. They needed this city to be under their rule, not in chaos like Paris had been.

So she pushed back the thoughts of unlocking the doors. She knew Jürgen would have her head if she messed this up. He was waiting for the opportunity to do her in, and she couldn't let him have that pleasure. Besides, she had realized her mistake—there was no redemption.

And the sounds of all the humans' shrieks fueled her hunger. Why had she run away all those decades ago? Why had she turned her back on this?

Licking the blood off her hand, she'd let her yellow catlike eyes take in the scene. Not a human soul was left—only empty shells that demons could now possess. Jürgen was in the back, treating this like a job and not showing any emotion on his face, but Gwen knew he loved doing stuff like this. As for James and Darrell, they both had wild smiles on their faces, just like Gwen. Blood was like catnip for them; even the smell could cause them to go into a frenzy. Luckily, if needed, they could hold that hunger back. Modern society made it harder for them to act on a whim as someone around could record what they did, and then they would be wanted criminals. They had learned how to adapt with the times though, and they'd never looked back.

But once Lucifer became the king of Earth, then they could do whatever they wanted whenever they wanted. Gwen couldn't wait.

Gwen licked the last drops of blood from her fingers as she walked up to the rest of the demons. "A new batch of minions. What a delight."

Darrell laughed. "I wish I'd seen you when you had a conscience. I still don't believe you ever felt anything for those Gargoyles. Not after what I've seen."

"What can I say? James is very persuasive when it comes to being a demon." She pulled James in and kissed him, gently biting his lip.

"Well, I won't forget." Jürgen's voice was steady. "And if anything you do suggests that you aren't back with us, I'll kill you."

Gwen rolled her eyes. "Like I haven't heard that one before."

Jürgen's fist came straight for her, but Gwen quickly grabbed it and flung him over her shoulder. Jürgen hit the floor with a loud thud. She bent down and placed her knee on his throat and whispered, "I have my powers back, my dear Jürgen. If you ever try to kill me, you will have another one coming. You got that?"

Jürgen glared at her, but she could see the smirk on the edge of his lips. She held him there in place, making sure he got the message. James and Darrell just stared at them, not wanting to get in the middle of their fight.

Jürgen shoved her off. "Now that is the Gwen I remember."

As the minions began to rise, Gwen wondered what was wrong with her mind as she felt a thought in the back of her mind get louder.

What would Collin think of her like this?

CHAPTER TWO

Collin

Collin took a deep breath of the crisp, fall air. Glancing up, he found the moon to be shining brightly in the dark sky. The city lights of Berlin didn't even diminish how much he could see of the night sky. Was this because of his new powers? Was he able to see everything clearly now, no matter how bright or dark it was? Letting out a breath, he wondered how he'd gotten into this mess. It really wasn't a question, as he knew the answer to all his problems—Guinevere.

She did this to him. She made him into a wretched

beast that now craved blood. He was no longer human but a creature not quite human, not quite demon. Collin clenched his hand. He hated her. He hated her so much. But, at the same time, deep down he knew he loved her. He didn't know why, but he did.

He could still remember her eyes the last time he saw her: bloodthirsty and demonic. James, her demon lover, stood behind her, smiling with satisfaction. He had ripped her back down to his level, and she was now in his grasp. James had tortured Gwen until she broke. Then she fulfilled her promise to Erik and made Collin into an unearthly creature.

Collin still wasn't sure if he was madder at Gwen or Erik for everything. Erik was just trying to use him to save the world, but Gwen had given Collin her blood when James tried to kill him years ago. It was all just a mess, and he would never go back to who he once was.

It had been weeks since he was changed, and they left London—the place he considered home. First Erik and Elizabeth had taken him to Vatican City where they let the church know they had lost a guardian of Heaven. Hugo, the Gargoyle he knew the best and had killed lesser demons with, was dead. He had been destroyed right in front of his eyes and right in front of Gwen, leaving only dust behind. He was now back in the stars where he was supposed to be.

After they'd finished their business in Vatican City, Collin used his vampire senses to figure out what direction the demons, more specifically Gwen, traveled. Now they were in Berlin, and the scent of Gwen hung in the air, no matter where Collin was.

Taking in another breath, Collin tried to locate where she was specifically. Sometimes he could pinpoint where she was, or sometimes the scent was masked by others—mainly James. Tonight was a night where he could sense a few demons, and they had stopped somewhere. Closing his eyes, he tried to focus.

They were in some kind of club, or at least in the district. After a few moments, a foul stench wafted in. Blood. So much of it filled the air, practically dampening it. Collin placed his hand over his mouth and nose to keep himself from inhaling. He craved blood more than anything in the world. Collin started coughing, his stomach churning at the thought of what he dearly yearned for. He could feel his eyes change, just as the other demons' did. It was a weird feeling, not describable in human terms. It was like a change in a way of seeing. A change of what could be seen—what he wanted to see.

Collin jumped down off the roof onto the balcony of their hotel room and entered, still coughing. Running toward the bathroom, he pushed up the toilet seat and watched as everything from the hours before came up.

Once he'd stopped vomiting, he turned the faucet on and splashed cold water on his face. He hadn't been able to hold anything down for the past week. At first he could eat normal food, but it was getting harder each and every day. The lack of food didn't make him weak, but the lack of blood did. He couldn't bring himself to do it though. He couldn't hurt a person like they did. He wasn't heartless. So he suffered and tried his best to find an alternative. So far, he had found nothing.

Looking up in the mirror, he saw Erik standing in the door behind him.

"How long have you been standing there?" Collin turned the faucet off.

"Long enough." Erik straightened up. "The smell still makes you sick?"

Collin nodded reluctantly.

"You will keep getting weaker until you drink blood."

He shook his head. "But I can't hold yours down. I

crave it and it makes me sick at the same time."

"I know."

"I can't take a human's either. I could never do it." Collin closed his eyes, thinking of minions he had seen Gwen feast on. He couldn't be a part of it—he couldn't bring himself to doing that. "I just need…" He stopped, knowing he shouldn't say the next word.

"Gwen's?"

Collin nodded. "She's here. I can sense her. They must have killed a lot of people because the smell of blood is strong."

"She is with the demons. James won't let you near her."

"You think I don't know that?" Collin yelled, then took a deep breath. "I'm sorry, it's just that I haven't had a good night's sleep in a while. All I dream of is blood, and I just need to calm myself down."

Erik nodded as he started to leave. "You know, I wouldn't blame you for going to her. It's just a matter of whether you want to face the consequences of trusting her."

Collin grinned half-heartedly. "And that's the question of the day, isn't it? Whether to trust her?"

Erik didn't say a word as he left him standing there.

Collin rubbed his temples as he walked over to the sliding glass door. He looked up at the moon once more and sighed.

"But what could she do that would make this worse?"

Erik murmured something under his breath, but Collin didn't catch what he said. He knew that the Gargoyles' run-in with Gwen over the years hadn't been that great, but something in her had changed—she wasn't the demon she once was. Then again, both the demons and Gargoyles pointed out many times that Collin hadn't known Gwen when she was in her full evil form. But they also didn't know her like he did—how tender and caring she could be. There was no way all of that was gone. It just couldn't be.

So the question was, why didn't he go find her? Although James was with her most of the time, he could get her alone. Was he worried that he would find out that she was indeed back to her demon ways? Or was he worried what he might do to her as he craved her blood far more than anything? Not only that, but he missed the way her lips felt on his, and her skin, and he began to wonder what it was like to pierce her skin with his own teeth.

He shook his head. No, he shouldn't think of such

things at a time like this. He needed to focus and help the Gargoyles. He couldn't let demons take over the world. He had to do something.

Which also meant that Gwen would have to eventually die. That thought always made it feel as if his heart was getting squeezed. She was his first real love, and the idea that she would be trapped in hell for the rest of her life was unbearable. There was no way she could go back to Heaven, as she had mentioned earlier, which was why no one trusted her wanting to help. She couldn't be redeemed. Granted, she'd turned her back on God himself. Collin still felt bad for her. He wondered what he would have done in her shoes. He didn't know.

The door to the hotel room opened, and both Erik and Collin turned to find Elizabeth walking in. She set her belongings to the side as she took off her sneakers.

"Well," Erik began. "What did you find?"

"It's what we expected." Elizabeth sighed. "They are making more and more minions. I am still not sure where they are going to attack first, but it will most definitely be soon."

"Why can't we just ambush them?" Collin asked. "I mean, we are able to locate. Couldn't we just surprise attack?"

Erik shook his head. "No, they can smell us like you can smell them. Also, there are more of them than us, and they could easily overtake us."

"If that is true, then why don't they just attack you two?"

Elizabeth answered, "Because they like to play games. They don't like to just take us out, they would rather play with their enemies like cats with mice. They enjoy to watching us suffer, and although they want the doors of hell to open, they also want to have a little fun with it."

"Which is why this has been going on for over two thousand years. And it's why we'll always be at an advantage—we aren't selfish."

After seeing the demons in action, Collin understood what they meant. They took pleasure in fighting and torturing. It would make sense that if they dragged it on this long, they were also having fun.

"So what do we now?" Collin asked.

"We watch and wait. And we deal with your cravings."

Elizabeth frowned. "Are they getting worse?"

Collin slowly nodded. "I can't keep anything down.

The air smells of blood… I just…" Collin turned away and collapsed on the sofa. "I'll need something soon or else I'm afraid I'll snap."

Elizabeth stepped up to Collin. "Do you want some of my blood?"

Collin shook his head. "No, it doesn't help. Erik gave me some earlier today, and I threw it up. I just need…" He sighed and got back up. "I'm going to bed. Thinking about this is only making it worse. I'll see you two in the morning."

Before either of them could protest and try to talk to him more, Collin closed his bedroom door and took a deep sigh as he smothered his face into his pillow.

CHAPTER THREE

James

James watched as his girl spun around in the moonlight, laughing at the success of creating more minions without a hitch. It was satisfying to see a smile on her face—a smile of true happiness. He didn't think he would ever see that face again, not after her betrayal. However, from what he could tell, she was truly back, and any thoughts of redemption were gone. She was the girl he'd fallen in love with.

Granted James was still pissed at her for leaving him behind and turning that human, but he couldn't help to be happy she was back and to have her blood on his lips once more. It also helped that he'd gotten to torture her until she broke. Only he was capable of bringing her back, and they both knew that. They were each other's weakness—something the Gargoyles now knew about. James just hoped that the secret they revealed to them wouldn't come back to bite them in the ass.

Jürgen and Darrell followed along as they all headed back to the hotel they were staying at. It was a luxurious hotel, as it always was. They weren't like the Gargoyles and looked for a cheap place to stay even though they could hypnotize humans. No, they liked to stay at places that were quite accommodating. They deserved it. That and the walls were quite thick, which James appreciated greatly.

Darrell grabbed Gwen's hand and twirled her around. "You're in a playful mood this evening."

Gwen spun herself around and started dancing with Darrell. "Indeed I am. I don't want this night to end."

Darrell spun her out, and James intervened by grabbing her and pulling her close. "And it doesn't have to, my love. Just say the word and this night will last forever."

She laughed, her cheeks cherrylike. "But where

would the fun in that be? Nothing would ever get done."

James ran his fingers against her neck. "Then what do you suppose we do to pass the time?"

Gwen bit her lip playfully. "I can think of a few things."

"Hm, maybe I don't want this night to end then." James kissed her gentle lips.

Darrell nudged Jürgen. "Why can't we have a relationship like that?"

Jürgen narrowed his eyes. "I do hope you mean with other people and not with each other."

Sadness overwhelmed Darrell's face. "You mean you don't love me?"

Jürgen threw a punch at him, and Darrell jumped back. He laughed. "You're so serious, Jürgen! Lighten up, will ya?"

"I'll lighten up when this war that should have been finished already is over. Meanwhile, I can be as stubborn as I want to be."

Gwen stuck her tongue out at Jürgen, who retaliated with his own tongue. Usually Jürgen didn't stoop so low as to stick his tongue out at someone, but it seemed Gwen always knew how to push his buttons.

James just laughed. "Just wait, Darrell. When the gates of hell are open, you can find yourself someone to love."

"Or," Gwen added, "you can find yourself a human. But they will probably leave you in the end."

James saw Jürgen glare at Gwen for a moment, then turn away. It seemed she was watching him for another reaction or comment, but he didn't say anything. James narrowed his eyes at Gwen, curious as to why she kept pushing his buttons and what buttons she was exactly pushing. It seemed to him that something had happened that they weren't talking about—something that happened decades before World War II. Gwen wasn't one to keep secrets from him, at least not back then. So what would this grudge be about? He made a mental note to bring it up later with her.

Darrell stretched his arms and leaned his head back into his hands. "Sorry, James, but even though I'm jealous of your relationship, there is no way I would risk a blood bond with someone like you have."

That comment brought James back out of his thoughts and into the present. Although he loved Gwen deeply and would do it all over again, he understood why no one else wanted to commit such an act. They were both weaker and stronger because of it. If it weren't for the fact that the two of them fell from Heaven for each other, he didn't know if he could have been so committed to anyone else.

Gwen, however, didn't take the comment lightly and slapped Darrell in the back of the head. "What is that supposed to mean?"

He rubbed the injury. "It means I wouldn't trust ya with my life. Sorry, Gwen, but you're too chaotic to ever want a blood bond with."

"Well." Gwen wrapped her arms around James. "Doesn't matter. I'm already taken. And there's no going back."

James smiled. There wasn't any going back; what was done was done. Gwen and he were tied forever, and they wanted it that way. They knew that the moment they had fallen to Earth. They performed a blood bond, making them connected throughout the rest of eternity. And no one could take that away, not even the hybrid Collin.

They kept on toward the hotel to get some rest before the festivities of the next day. They were almost ready to attack the ministry. German politics were now a bit more complicated to tweak and corrupt. That was why they have been turning groups upon groups of people each night—that way they could infiltrate the common people before they attack them. No one would protest the changes that were about to come—the changes that would turn the world against God himself. The Gargoyles wouldn't be able to do a thing except watch as the humans became more and more corrupt by the minions that were in charge. Then they would end the last Gargoyles and be able to open the gates to hell.

And Lucifer could once again walk on Earth.

They were almost to the hotel when they passed by a church. A young man, looking no older than Gwen appeared to look, was huddled on the steps with a sign. Gwen bent down to read the sign with a grin on her lips.

"Interesting," Gwen whispered as she licked her lips. "The end is near, you say?"

"Yes, miss, the end is coming. Are you ready for it?" the young man asked.

James watched as Gwen's lips curled into a smile. "Am I ready? Ah, poor boy…" Her eyes flashed yellow. "I'll be the one to bring the end. Question is, are you ready?"

The boy's eyes widened as he scrambled to get up

and run for his life. He scraped his hands, and the scent of blood filled James's nostrils. His own eyes flashed yellow as the hunger rose. Even after their feast, he was still hungry for more. Peering over to Jürgen and Darrell, he saw that they felt the same.

A little hunt never hurt.

Gwen yelled out into the night as the boy ran for his life. "I'll count to ten, so you better find a nice place to hide!"

Gwen always did love to play with her food. James smiled at that thought as he wrapped his arms around her and kissed her.

"I love you and your sadistic mind," James said.

She bit her lip. "We'll see if you say that later tonight."

Darrell made gagging noises as Gwen started counting. "One! Two! Three!"

James could hear the boy crying as he ran farther down the streets. It wouldn't matter how far he ran or where he tried to hide—with that injury, they would be able to track him down wherever he went. Gwen was simply playing one of her games.

"Four! Five! Six!"

The boy was trying to open locked store doors.

Luckily no housing developments were around her but simply some shops. At least for how far he was able to run in ten seconds.

"Seven! Eight!"

James wondered if Gwen was going to run at a normal speed or use her demon powers to be in front of the boy in seconds. He glanced to Jürgen and Darrell and saw the hunger on their faces. More than likely, she was going to use her demon powers to make sure she beat the two of them to the fresh meal. Question was, would he also run to the boy just to play with Gwen, or would she let him feed in peace? The answer, of course, was the latter.

"Nine! Ten!"

All four of them sped to where the man was slamming his hand on a door, hoping someone was around to help him. No one would save him, however. That made James smile as he watched the human scramble back, hitting his head on the door, tears running down his face.

"Please, don't," the boy pleaded. He was shaking, and the wound had bled even more, the savory scent filling the air. Jürgen stood behind Gwen and Darrell, pacing back and forth. This boy had no chance of surviving the night. They would not recognize the body in the morning—if they even found one.

Gwen raised an eyebrow. "Don't what?"

"Don't kill me." His voice was barely audible as he was shaking.

James licked his lips.

Gwen bent down to the boy, who held out his hands as if they would stop her. She smiled. "But you said the end was coming, so why would it matter if I just kill you now?"

"Because I have so much to live for."

Gwen shook her head as she grabbed his collar. "No, no you don't."

Gwen bit his neck as the boy screamed out. His scream died down as his soul left his body. Now all that was left was an empty carcass that could turn into a minion or be devoured. For this boy, it would be the latter.

James stepped up to Gwen and the body and grabbed his arm. Pulling up his sleeve, James bit into the skin, letting the sweet taste of blood fill his mouth. Nothing compared to the taste of blood, especially the blood of an innocent fool. Well, that wasn't exactly true, as Gwen's blood was sweeter than anyone else's, but besides hers, this was a close second.

"Hey!" Jürgen interrupted. "It's our turn to feast."

James backed away as Gwen let go with a chuckle. "So demanding. Fine. Here you two go. Leave nothing behind."

Gwen chucked the body at Darrell and Jürgen, who immediately devoured the blood that was left, ripping his limbs and getting every drop that they could. Blood stained the pavement in a color that James loved—a red that only creatures of the night could fully enjoy.

"Last to reach their fill has to clean up the mess," Gwen called out as she grabbed James's hand and started running, leading him away from the scene.

"Hey!" Jürgen called out. "Get back here! This is your mess!"

Gwen peered back and stuck out her tongue at them as they turned down a street, now out of Jürgen's and Darrell's view. She was laughing, the sweet sound music to James's ears. He wanted to make her smile and laugh like that each and every day. Once they opened the gates of hell, he knew that would be possible.

After they reached a good distance from the others, Gwen turned around to him with a serious look. He realized she made the distraction so they could speak privately. James raised an eyebrow.

"What's wrong?"

She took in a deep breath and let out slowly. "The Gargoyles used their salt to mask themselves, but I can sense Collin. They are in the city."

James furrowed his eyebrows. "Seth didn't think they would be able to follow us so soon."

Gwen laughed. "As if he has ever been right for anything."

"Fair point. What should we do? We should probably tell Jürgen and Darrell."

She nodded. "Yes, but I also don't want to hear their shit about the Gargoyles being able to follow me because of a mistake I made. Besides, it seems he left their hideout and is heading toward us."

James knew she meant Collin. He folded his arms. "Then what do you propose we do?"

She leaned in and kissed him. "We play our little game of course."

CHAPTER FOUR

Erik

Erik watched as Collin jumped off the balcony outside his room and headed into the night. Erik let out the long-awaited sigh and pinched the bridge of his nose. It wasn't going according to plan. Nothing ever went according to plan. Collin was supposed to sustain energy from their blood so he wouldn't have to worry about Gwen corrupting it. He slammed his fist into the wall, careful not to punch through it.

"That bad, eh?" Erik turned to find Elizabeth standing behind him. She had a worried look about her.

Erik shrugged. "Just don't know how this is all going to play out."

"But he needs to see her; it could help him."

"Or she could make it worse and torture him mentally."

Elizabeth didn't answer. She knew he was right. Gwen was a wildcard, and if she was anything like she was before World War II, she would make some sadistic game out of it—just like she warned.

Erik rested his head on the wall. "I just don't know if we should have let him go alone."

She placed her hand on his shoulder. "They wouldn't let him near if we were with him, and you know that. They can sense us if we don't have the right protection."

"I know that. I just feel bad for making him face her alone, especially after all the things she has done in the past."

"His past, or your past?"

Erik frowned. He didn't want to think about all the things Gwen had done to him through the years. How he could even trust her in London like he did was beyond him. Maybe it was the fear in her eyes, or maybe it was his own soft heart. Or maybe it was because he needed her to change Collin. Whatever it was caused Hugo to lose his life on Earth and he wouldn't forgive himself for that. He never would forgive her for that.

"I can't forgive her for the things she had done to me and Hugo, but we both know Collin isn't taking the change very well, and she may be the only one to get him on track." Erik saw Elizabeth tense when he mentioned Hugo's name. The two of them had always been close. "I'm sorry I brought up Hugo."

"It's fine. It just happened so fast. We shouldn't have trusted her."

"I know, but Hugo was the one who agreed to the risk. He knew he could die because of it. It's all part of war."

"War," she repeated and kicked a chair, surprising Erik. He rarely saw her lash out in such a way. "I am sick of that word. I'm so sick of all this."

Erik nodded in agreement. "So am I, to be honest. We weren't destined to be on Earth this long."

"Weren't we though? Is this not our destiny?"

Erik knew she had a point. The God that they serve knew everything that was, is, and will be. He knew how this would end, so the Gargoyles were there for a reason. They would have to succeed, otherwise they wouldn't be sent.

"You are right," Erik commented. "We'll win. We have to."

Elizabeth shrugged. "Would it matter in the end? The demons will probably figure something else out to cause us trouble. They always do. They haven't just been a problem in recent centuries but even in Heaven before they were cast out. There will never be rest when they still exist somewhere."

Erik furrowed his brows. "What are you suggesting?"

"I am suggesting we smite them from existence. Get rid of any traitors and live in peace." She slammed her fist on the table. "For once, we can have peace."

Erik sighed. "You know that would never happen. It isn't up to us. This is the way He commands it."

"I know." She rubbed her forehead. "I just wish we could though. I don't want to deal with their kind any longer."

Erik knew she was right. If they could just destroy the demons from existence, there would be no more suffering—there would be no more war. They could live in peace and not have to be at war constantly. But that wasn't how life worked. That wasn't how the universe was meant to be. They had to live with what cards were laid out before them even if the deck itself was lousy.

Elizabeth turned to face him. "What should we do if Collin can't handle the change? What if his body rejects it completely?"

He didn't even want to think about that. Even though it was Gwen's and James's fault that he was brought back to life, Erik had forced Gwen to turn him into a full hybrid—a human with demonic powers. If Collin couldn't work out the change, Erik would feel responsible. No, he had to work it out. He had to solve it. This was their last hope in bringing this war to a close.

It also didn't help that there were five generals of Lucifer left on Earth and only two of them. With Collin, there were three. The odds were against them, but Erik would never give up hope. Hope was the only thing they had left.

Erik sighed. "It won't. Gwen will figure out a way to keep him going. She won't want her fun to end so soon."

Elizabeth took a seat. "I guess the question is not whether he will live due to not being able to process our blood but whether he will be able to take the mental torment that she will cause."

Erik sat down across from her. "She's changed. I don't think she will hurt him like she once hurt us."

She shook her head. "You don't actually believe that. Do you not remember when she nailed your body and wings to the top of the pyramids and let you sweat in the sun for thirty days? Or the time she tied you to an anchor on their ship and let you drown every time they were at a harbor? How she chained you down and watch as she slaughtered your brothers and sisters one by one, ripping them into pieces until her bloodlust was satisfied?"

Erik turned away. Of course he remembered. It was still all too vivid, and it was why he didn't trust Gwen in the first place. If it hadn't been for Collin, he would have killed her on the spot. But they needed the extra member even if it was such a gamble.

"I remember. And I know she has nothing to gain by helping us. But Collin is a strong human. He has fought many minions, and I think he could be our ticket to taking them down. And although I care for humans, losing one to his sanity isn't a large price to pay—not when he will still be able to go to Heaven after all this is over."

Elizabeth frowned, but she knew he had a point. What was one human's life compared to the fate of the world? She slowly nodded. "Right. We'll remember that going forward. We'll stop worrying and keep an eye on him to make sure he doesn't betray us."

Erik nodded in agreement. "Right. That is what we'll do. For the world. We can't lose each other or else I fear neither of us will succeed in defeating them on our own."

"We'll put up a fight to the end."

CHAPTER FIVE

Collin

Collin paced outside the hotel complex. Back and forth his feet shuffled as he ran his hands through his hair again and again. It was a mistake being there, and he knew it. Stopping, he sighed as he looked up at the building before him. It was his only chance to pick up the pieces she left for him. He needed answers, and she had them.

Earlier they had been all around Berlin, gathering minions, or at least that was what Collin figured. He could smell a lot of blood in the air as it lingered like the sweet scent of flowers in spring. He wished he could do something to block the scent as it made his mouth water.

The only thing he could do was go up and confront Gwen.

Stepping inside, he didn't need to ask the front desk what room she was in. He could tell. He could sense her all around the city. Still not sure if that was a good or bad thing, Collin pressed the third floor—the top floor—and watched as the world in front of him vanished.

The soft sound of music filled his ears as the elevator took him up the floors. It wasn't long before he arrived to the floor and the doors chimed open. He stepped out and headed down the hall.

Fifth door from the end.

Collin held his fist for a moment, hesitant to face Gwen. She was the one who made him this way, and he still blamed her for everything even though it was his decision. He told her he could handle it—that he wanted to be able to help the Gargoyles. But now that he was a hybrid, he understood why she didn't want to change him. The thirst was agonizing, and the way he could sense blood in the air like it was a sweet perfume made him not understand who he was anymore. Having been a human who didn't have these cravings to now being something that wasn't quite evil but was most definitely not human kept him up at night.

Giving up on wanting to get answers, he knocked. He could hear Gwen's sweet laughter as she opened the door. Her brown eyes stared at him with such excitement, and her red hair was messed up and yet perfect. All she had on was James's button-up shirt. Her long legs extended from his baggy shirt, long and exquisite. He remembered how soft her skin was when she was in his hands. Now James had his hands around her, keeping a steady eye on Collin as he stood there.

Gwen looked amused yet surprised at the same time. "Collin, I didn't expect you would actually knock. I thought I would have to open the door and force you to come in."

"I need… to talk to you." Collin couldn't say the words. What he really needed was her blood, but he couldn't come out and say that. He feared she would make fun of him, but he had a feeling she knew why he was there. It was obvious.

She chuckled as she moved herself and James out of the doorway. "Then by all means, come in."

Collin stepped inside, surprised at how elaborate the

room was. Historic German reprints littered the wall with vases and sculptures spread across the area. A large sectional couch encircled the fireplace that was lit. The flames roared away as Gwen and James sat down. Collin hesitated, wondering if he should also sit down. He decided to take a seat in the chair that was farthest from James as he didn't like the look he was getting from him.

"So…" Gwen reached for a glass of red liquid that sat on the table before her. "What brings you here?"

"Please tell me that is wine." Collin watched as she took a sip of it, the dark red tinting her lips.

She laughed. He missed her laugh and all the times that she was at his pub. This felt a bit different, however, as if she was showing her true, darker nature in her mannerisms.

"Of course it is. You would be able to tell if it wasn't." She raised the glass. "Do you care for some?"

Collin shook his head. "No, I'm all right."

Her lips twisted in a sly smile. "I meant blood."

James shot her a look, as if he didn't like the idea of her sharing his blood with Collin.

Collin gulped, realizing that there was no way James was going to let her give him what he needed. He was a fool for thinking that he could meet up with her when he was around. The problem was that Collin never sensed James was away from Gwen for even a brief moment. He was surprised the other two he sensed weren't nearby. Perhaps they had other business to take care of.

Collin's hands began to shake. "I… don't…"

"Gwen, sweetheart." James stroked the side of her face down to her chin. "What are you doing?"

She turned to him with a pout on her face. "Can't you see the poor boy's hungry?"

He twirled her hair with his finger. "Yes, but I'd rather kill him than let him…"

"James," Gwen snapped. "Leave me alone with him." She batted her eyes. "Please?"

His eyes narrowed. "Had you said this was your plan tonight, I would not have agreed."

She smiled and leaned in to kiss him on the mouth. Collin looked away as they kissed harder. It was apparent that Gwen was using her femininity to get what she wanted from James. Collin didn't much appreciate seeing his ex, if that was the right term in this arrangement, making out with the guy who had attempted to kill him.

They stopped and James let out a sigh. "Fine. I'll let you have your fun. But you will owe me, Guinevere."

She blew him a kiss as he left to their bedroom and closed the door. Gwen turned back to Collin. "So that is why you're here then? Are the cravings that bad?"

Collin fiddled with his hands. He didn't want to have to explain why he was there, but he knew it must be done. "I can't hold anything down, blood nor food."

"You can't hold any blood down? Not even the Gargoyles?"

He shook his head. "No. Neither of theirs."

"Now that's interesting." She stood up and stoked the fire. "Interesting indeed."

Collin furrowed his brows. "Why?"

"Because the last one I created didn't have that problem. I wonder what it could be. Perhaps you're too kind and your mind is rejecting the idea of blood."

"Can you blame me? Besides, didn't you once go without blood for a long time?"

She straightened up, her strong eyes watching his. "You think it has to do with…? As you probably noticed, I no longer have problems with human blood."

"You did."

She shrugged. "Perhaps, but my body didn't reject it.

It definitely didn't reject Gargoyle blood nor minion blood. I could take that without thinking twice. I presume the Gargoyles have tried using it themselves."

"It worked at first but nothing beyond the third or fourth time."

"Fascinating." She stepped over and placed each of her legs on either side of him and settled down on his lap.

"What are you—?" Collin began as she smiled.

She moved her short hair to one side. "Go ahead then, see if it will make you sick."

Collin gazed at her neck, every urge in his body telling him it was the right thing. He could feel his eyes turn yellow in hunger—the same color as the demons'. He moved closer to her neck but shook his head and pushed her off him.

"I can't." He stood up and walked to the window. "I can't do this."

Gwen wrapped her arms around him. "Yes, you can, Collin. Just do what your body commands you to do."

He missed the feeling of her arms. He knew it was wrong, as she was already taken, and in a deeper sense than any human could understand. But it felt so good. He turned to face her. "I don't feel like I'll be able to stop."

"Well, you won't know until you try." She bit her lip. "If you're afraid of hurting me, believe me, you won't."

Collin let out a laugh. "I'm not afraid of hurting you."

"Really?" She lifted her hand and sliced the base of her neck with her nails. Blood rolled down her collarbone. She placed her finger that had a dark red drop of blood to his lips. "Try to resist hurting me now."

Collin just stared at the dark redness that began to cover her skin and soak the shirt she wore. He tried to fight it, but seeing it there, in front of him, he couldn't resist.

Wrapping his arms around her, he pulled her close and sank his fangs into her skin. He felt the rush of energy as it entered his body. Nothing in the world could compare. He felt alive again—in fact, he felt more than alive. He felt as if he were unstoppable.

"Little lost puppy, that is what you are, Collin," she whispered into his ear. "Don't know where to go, don't know who to trust. A new world is open to you, and you don't know where to take the first step."

Collin backed away from her. "Are you mocking

me?"

"Why, yes I am. You're so afraid, Collin." She placed her hand on the side of his face. "Don't let that fear stop you from doing what you want to do. What your instincts tell you to do." Gwen leaned in even closer and whispered, "Take whatever you want. Nothing can stop you."

He shouldn't have come. Collin's heart began to race. He craved more blood, and he began to feel as if he didn't care where it came from.

"I have to get out of here." He fumbled toward the door and went into the hallway, stumbling against the wall as he made his way to the elevator. He entered, and as the doors began to close, a hand stopped them. Gwen stepped in.

"You didn't think you could just come and take what you want without giving something back, did you?"

"What do you mean?"

She licked her lips as her eyes turned yellow. "My blood for yours."

Collin took a breath as she bit into his neck. The memory flooded back to him of last time she bit him. James had driven her over the edge, filling her heart with hate once more. Now she was trying to do the same with him.

He didn't feel the pain as he did earlier, more just a pinch that was gone the second her fangs were into his neck. He admitted it felt different this time. This time he wanted her to take his blood. This time he felt as if there was a connection.

Gwen released moments later, only taking a tiny bit of his blood. He doubted she needed it with James at her side but more just to put him in his place. He didn't mind though. It felt rather good.

"Next time I don't want your blood but something else in return. Information perhaps?" She leaned in and kissed him playfully, licking the excess blood off his lips. "Keep that in mind, all right?"

He watched as she stepped out of the elevator and back toward where James awaited. The doors shut, and he pushed the button to the main floor. Leaning back against the wall, he slid down onto the floor, head between his legs, thinking of what to do next. He felt her grasp around his thoughts, and he didn't know if he really wanted to resist it.

CHAPTER SIX

Gwen

Gwen smiled gleefully as she skipped back to her hotel room. Things went exactly how she wanted, and Collin's mind was wrapped around her beautiful little finger. It would be fun to make him crack, not to mention how much information she might get from him about the Gargoyles. Watching them be destroyed by the very thing they made her create would be the cherry on top.

As Gwen stepped inside and closed the door behind her, she found James standing in the middle of the room, arms crossed and eyes glaring.

"What's wrong with you?"

"Seriously?" His eyes looked as if they were going to flame. He waved his arm up. "What the hell are you thinking? Why are you giving him your blood?"

She sighed. "James, don't act like a jealous boyfriend. He means nothing to me." Gwen let the word *nothing* linger on her lips.

He laughed. "Oh really? Then kill him right now." His voice was still raised.

Gwen stepped up to him. "But where would be the fun in that?"

He shook his head. "I don't care about the fun. I care about him sucking your neck."

She placed her hand on his cheek. "Dearest, you're the only one for me. Don't you want to make him suffer?"

Her flirting didn't work on him. "Yes, but I don't like sharing."

Gwen laughed. That was definitely true; she had learned that through the years.

"But think of all the things we could make him do." Gwen ran her fingers through James's hair. "Get him to turn on the Gargoyles and such."

"What if he doesn't turn on them?"

"Then I'll kill him." She raised an eyebrow. "Satisfied?"

James smiled as he wrapped his arms around her waist. "A little bit. So long as you promise me if he compromises anything, you will rip his heart out yourself."

"I'll even deliver it to you on a silver platter."

"Now I like the sound of that." He kissed her lips slowly, then backed away. "Meanwhile, we need to figure out what's next in order to take this country down."

She watched as he stopped in front of the balcony. "Really? You want to talk work now?"

"Dawn is already here—we need to act fast. We can't screw this up."

Gwen wrapped her arms around him and started to slip her fingers under his shirt. "So soon? Here I thought we could get some more alone time."

James didn't budge. "You had your fun. Now go wash up. We are meeting the others soon."

She paused for a moment, surprised at how serious he'd become. James had never said no to her, not in the thousands of years they had been together. It couldn't have been Collin. She had played games with many men through the years. At least she didn't think it could be.

Sighing, she decided not to push it. Entering the bathroom, she turned the shower on to warm up and pulled off the blood-soaked shirt. Something had been bothering James since they had arrived to Germany. He never talked about it, but she could tell.

James still loved her. Gwen knew that. He forgave her for her screwup, and she trusted he meant that when he said so. He knew she loved him with all her heart. So what was bothering him?

Gwen stepped into the shower and let the hot water rinse away the blood on her hands. She loved the feeling water always gave her. It felt as if everything she had done just vanished down the drain. It was soothing and refreshing. It would be all she had to keep her head up and away from the bloodshed she stepped in.

There was no use getting upset about everything that happened. James was right. She couldn't turn back. She would have to live with everything she had done and move on. She was a demon, and there was no changing that. There was no changing what one was; one just had to live with it.

She shut the water off and stepped out of the shower. James was already dressed and waiting for her in the bedroom. She gathered her clothes and put them on. She wore her typical multilayered tank top with jeans and boots. She would grab a leather jacket to go over it, as per norm. As she put on her clothes, she eyed James, wondering why he never mentioned that they were meeting in the morning. Did he still not trust her? Forgiveness and trust were two completely different things—they would know. Would she ever earn that trust back? Did she deserve for him to trust her again?

Part of her didn't want to know that answer, but another part of her wanted to know what was going through his head. Maybe she did take everything with Collin too far, but it had been his fault. If James hadn't killed him in the first place, she wouldn't have had to bring him back. And it was James who bargained with the Gargoyles and made her turn him. If she ever brought any of that up, however, he would just say it was her fault for running off in the first place. He wasn't wrong though.

"Are you ready? Jürgen and Darrell should be waiting for us at the base."

Gwen rolled her eyes. "Why do we need a base if we're staying at a hotel? Why can't we just hang out at the hotel and talk?"

"Because people can overhear us easily."

She laughed. "That didn't seem to stop us from talking about other things. And doing other things."

A smirk appeared on James's face. "We're just taking extra precautions. We don't want to mess up again."

"You mean for them to be mad at me even more."

James's face tightened. "I mean… Well, yes."

"Well, I know Darrell trusts me and is fine with me being around. Seth, well, I always get on his bad side no matter what I do. He's jealous, if you ask me. And Jürgen, well…"

"I have been meaning to ask about what happened between the two of you. The three of us used to be best buds, but a few centuries ago, his attitude changed a bit."

Gwen forgot she never told him about the incident. This wasn't the time, however, to rehash old memories. "Didn't you say we were going to be late? We should probably get going."

He smiled as he gestured to the door. "After you. But don't think that this conversation is over. I tried to bring it up with Jürgen, but he wasn't talking."

"Then maybe you should let it go."

"Right, as if you have ever let anything go."

She laughed as they headed into the elevator and down to the main level where her bike awaited. Gwen climbed on her black 1940 BMW R75 motorbike after James. She took in a deep breath of the exhaust as James cranked on the gas. She missed riding with him and was glad she could wrap her arms around him once more.

Even if that came at the cost of her sanity.

The sun's light stretched across the city, bringing the early risers up and out of bed. A few people walked on the sidewalks next to them as they rode by, mostly businessmen heading to work. A few late-night partiers stumbled back to their home to finally head to bed or get ready for work. It was nothing a little coffee couldn't fix.

Gwen peered around. Berlin had changed over the years, but she still remembered it like it was yesterday. Red and black filled the streets, marching through and through. This country gained control of everything around it. People united together for one cause: to bring what they considered order to the world around them, and there was nothing that would have stopped them.

Except for her.

They had the Gargoyles in their grasp—their plan was flawless; she made sure of it. Except then she'd sabotaged all of it and brought the country and the victory of the war down with her. Then she ran for almost a century, hiding and making sure they couldn't find her. But alas, James did and now here she was, back in his arms.

Did she regret sabotaging everything? She didn't know the answer to that. The fact that everyone blamed her for everything did make her regret it, but the thought of opening the gates of hell still frightened her. She served Lucifer, yes, but she didn't like the idea of letting his destruction come to Earth. If he was allowed on the streets of this world, he would wreak havoc, and all the things she loved would be gone.

But now she didn't have a choice and had to help open the gates of hell. Why? Well, otherwise she would be tortured for eternity by the big man himself. That wasn't something she looked forward to. So if she brought hell on Earth, there would be no torture. Just an eternity with James.

When they arrived to the hideout, which was in a

building near Alexanderplatz, Darrell and Jürgen were already waiting for them. Gwen wondered if they even slept or if they spent the morning hours disposing of the body. More than likely it was the latter, Gwen knew.

Jürgen raised an eyebrow as they approached. "You're here on time?"

"We have things to get done, don't we? It's now or never," James answered.

Gwen fidgeted with her coat sleeve. Jürgen was right. They never were on time. Something was still bothering James, and she didn't want to think about it.

"Good to see you have your priorities straight for once." Jürgen turned and entered the building.

James followed, and before Gwen could step in behind him, Darrell pulled her aside. "What's wrong?"

"What do you mean?"

He shook his head. "James looks serious, and you guys got here on time. I thought after last night, you two would have been late."

She shrugged. "I don't know." She glanced inside where James was already sitting at the table. "I really don't know."

CHAPTER SEVEN

James

James watched as Darrell pulled Gwen aside. It wasn't that odd. Darrell and her talked all the time. They were close. But the way she glanced at him made James know that it was about him.

Gwen wasn't blind. She knew something was bothering him, and she was right. He was glad to have her back. He was happy to see her smiling face. He forgave her for hurting him and stabbing him in the back.

But he didn't feel he could trust her any longer.

Everything she did made him start to worry she would turn on him again. Everything with Collin. Everything with the Gargoyles. He knew that at any moment she could run away and try to stop their fate. It didn't seem to be the case; it didn't seem like it was going to happen. But there weren't any warnings the first time. He was caught completely by surprise, and he was heartbroken she would betray him like that. So although he trusted her when she said she loved him more than she cared about that human, he couldn't help but wonder if they were planning something or if she was going to use Collin to destroy any chance they had in bringing forth Lucifer himself.

Granted, Lucifer could come to this world every once in a while to check in—if he had enough power—but that wasn't the same as having free rein. He only was able to come to Earth once a century, and the last time he'd shown his face to them was before World War II. Now that James thought about it, he might have enough power to come back here soon. He didn't look forward to that. Hopefully by then they will have opened the doors. Otherwise, he had a feeling he was going to take out his frustrations on Gwen.

James tried to shake the thoughts out of his head, but

they still sat there in the back of his mind, nagging at him. If they didn't succeed now, it would be her fault. She would be the one they blamed. She would be the one they tortured. He couldn't allow that. He couldn't stand by and let it happen. He had to make this work. They had to succeed this time. So that was why he didn't want to goof around. He wanted to show everyone they were serious.

Gwen and Darrell finally stepped inside and took a seat at the table. Files were already pulled out for their next task. Jürgen pushed in a few keys on the laptop, and Seth appeared on the screen. A slight smirk was already plastered on his face, and he brought his fingers into a steeple.

"Good morning, Seth," Gwen chimed. "I see you're in a good mood."

"Yes, because for once things are going to plan. Germany will be ours soon, and we'll win this war," he explained as he shifted in his chair. "It's only a matter of time before the gates of hell are open and we'll reap what we have fought so hard for."

"Destruction?" Gwen licked her lips in excitement.

"Exactly. All we need to do is make sure everything keeps going according to plan." Seth eyed Gwen. "And

I do mean everything."

"Don't worry. I have everything under control. The hybrid will bring us information about the Gargoyles, and we'll be able to use their so-called wildcard against them."

James stared at her but said nothing. She wanted to believe she had Collin under control, but he knew she didn't. Collin was with the Gargoyles. He should be killed. He had a stronger conscience than the others. He would be able to hold himself against her even though she could be persuasive. Then there was also the problem of keeping Gwen under control.

He doubted she really wanted to go back to where she was, running and hiding from them. But James couldn't get that nagging feeling to go away. She could run out that door at any second, and he would have to hunt her down all over again. No, she wouldn't do it, not this far in the game. Then he remembered how close they had been to winning the last time, and uncertainty began to fill his heart once again.

"Oh yeah?" Jürgen chimed in. "Then how did last night go?"

Gwen shot Jürgen a look. She didn't want Seth to know that Collin had visited them. Jürgen must have sensed his smell in the air.

"He is breaking. I let him know if he ever shows his face again, he better bring me information."

"And how do you know he will be back?" Seth asked. "If he is loyal to the Gargoyles, he won't be back."

Gwen smiled. "Because he can't stomach any other blood than my own. He is wrapped around my well-manicured finger." She held up her hand to show off her black fingernail polish. He had to admit, it was his favorite color on her.

Seth's eyes widened. "He can't stomach any other blood? No other hybrid has ever had that problem."

"So he will come back for you," Jürgen added. "You actually succeed in something this time, Guinevere."

Gwen stuck her tongue out at him. "As I said, I always know what I am doing."

"Yeah… Right…," Jürgen said. "Just like last time. His dependency on you can end in two ways. Either he gives us the information we need or you will fall for the sad little puppy eyes and betray us again. You might have James and Darrell fooled, but Seth and I know your game. We know you can't be trusted."

James and her met eyes, and she appeared a little

sorrowful. She probably knew that was why he had been acting cold to her, but he couldn't help it. Jürgen was right. She couldn't be trusted.

"Jürgen has a point," Seth said. "How do we know you won't betray us again?"

Gwen bit her lip. She didn't like where this was going. She knew it was her fault though. If she hadn't betrayed them, they wouldn't be in this mess.

"I won't betray you. I learned my lesson. There is no redemption for us, and the Gargoyles just used me and made me do the one thing I didn't want to do."

Seth laughed. "You always knew there was no redemption, and you expected the Gargoyles to use you. Your reasoning doesn't make us suspect you any less."

Before Gwen said anything, James interjected. "Don't worry. I won't let history repeat itself. She won't betray us for a second time. I can guarantee it."

"That's what you always say, James. I can't help but think that perhaps you're blindsided by that blood bond of yours."

James clenched his jaw. Although he didn't like it, Seth had a point. Gwen could use him with the blood bond, not to mention he did have feelings for her.

Jürgen spoke before James could respond. "I'll make

sure the two of them don't cause trouble. As you see, they showed up on time today. I have a feeling they will be on their best behavior from now on."

"Good. That is what I like to hear." Seth seemed to be gathering things on his desk. "As for the next step, Jürgen has already put together files you are to take care of. After that, you can aim for the ministry. All your minions, all your force. Take them down. We're almost done here, and after that you will all meet up with me in Moscow."

"Understood," James said.

The Zoom call ended. James was still impressed that humans figured out all this technology so fast and how one company will be the leading force for a while, then it would change to a different one. It was so strange how human businesses were run. Either way though, it was handy for them. They didn't have to wait long periods of time for letters or have to travel a great distance. Granted, they could use their superspeed, but it wasn't as satisfying.

James turned to Jürgen. "So what do you have in store for us next?"

"Well." Jürgen opened his own file. "Darrell and I are going to take the tower in downtown. It's owned by a railroad company."

"That could come in handy," Gwen commented.

"Yes, we'll turn every person in the building into a minion. You and James can take Bundesdruckerei. They are in charge of bank notes, passports, and driver's licenses."

"Good. I need a new passport and ID." Gwen pulled out a card. It was an off-white with the East German insignia stamped on it. A black-and-white photo of her was plastered on one side. "Mine's a little old."

"I'd say." Darrell grabbed the card and examined it. "Your hair was a disaster."

Gwen gave him a look and then smiled. Slowly but steadily she began to tap her hand on the table. Darrell just stared at her. She did it again and again until she had a good rhythm going. Darrell looked at her with fear as she repeated the beat over and over again. Finally he grabbed her arms.

"Stop it! All right, I'm sorry! Just stop." He placed his hands over his ears. "No more drums."

Gwen laughed as she stuck her ID back into her pocket. "Well then, shall we?"

CHAPTER EIGHT

Erik

Erik watched as Collin stumbled inside the hotel room as the sun rose, his collar tainted with blood. His lips still had a tint of red, and he appeared disheveled. He was breathing heavily, as if he ran back there, which he probably did. Gwen must have let him drink and took his blood in return, just because she could. She didn't need it, as they had been feeding on humans all this time, not to mention she was back with James. She did it to frighten him and for him to know his place.

And because she liked to play games.

Gwen had been at Erik's throat more than once. Excluding when he let her drink his blood in London, she managed to drink his blood a total of twenty times over the centuries. It was a miracle that Erik was still alive. Lucky for him, Gwen loved to play games more than she wanted to get work done. He was able to get away each time but not without the help of another Gargoyle. Now that only Elizabeth was left, his fear of what she might do to him grew.

No, he was a servant of God. He did not fear her. He would not fear a demon.

Collin collapsed on the ground on his hands and knees, still trying to take deep breaths. He was a hybrid and shouldn't have been so weak after a run. It was apparent this was a panic attack.

Erik sat down on the floor next to him and placed his hand on his back. "Want to talk about it?"

Collin shook his head. "No, I'd rather not."

"Well, if you change your mind, I'm always here. Otherwise, do you want to rest? Dawn has already come, but I would understand if you want to…"

"No, I want to get this over with. I want to make her pay for what she did to me." Collin stood up. "What is our next plan of action?"

Erik saw the pain in his eyes. Whatever happened, Collin wasn't going to talk. Erik recalled all the things Gwen did to him in the past. Torture, pain, death. It was all a game for her enjoyment. Now she had Collin to play with, and Erik couldn't even imagine what she had in store for him—he couldn't imagine what she had in store for all of them. He should have never let her live. Instead of making her change Collin, he should have ripped out her heart right then and there. Had he known about the blood bond with James, he just might have, as James would have been weak, and they could have killed him. Then it would only have been three against three. Those odds wouldn't have been too bad.

But that was a lot of what-ifs, and there was no point thinking about them. He had to mentally stay in the present and focus on what they were going to do. He couldn't let past events deter him. What was happening in the present was the only way to change the future.

Elizabeth stepped out of the bathroom, already changed into her daily T-shirt and jeans. She dried her hair with the towel as she glanced over at Collin. She appeared as if she were about to say something, but Erik shook his head. Elizabeth nodded, understanding that Collin did not want to talk.

"Well, first," Erik began. "We should get you cleaned up. Take a nice shower to clear your head, and then we'll go over our next plan."

Elizabeth nodded. "Right. Don't think this city is lost because of all the minions. We had a plan of action put in place long before the demons came back to Berlin."

Collin stood up. "What do you mean?"

"After Germany fell in World War II, we made sure nothing like it would ever happen here again. We contacted every chancellor from then on out in Germany. They knew there had to be something behind the war and listened to us. They have known about the Twelve and what they are capable of. Every time they meet they make sure no minions are among them," Elizabeth explained.

"How do they do that?"

"Silver," Erik answered. "They pass around a silver cup to make sure no one has been turned. They are cautious about anyone who comes near the ministry."

"But now this is the war front. There needs to be action before Gwen and the others attack. Just checking for minions isn't going to do them any good if they come straight to them and massacre everyone."

"But first go wash up. You need to calm down and

focus," Erik said as he stood up.

Collin nodded. "You are right. Thank you."

Collin headed into the bathroom, and once the shower was on and he couldn't hear the two of them, Elizabeth spoke.

"What do you think happened?"

Erik shrugged as he collapsed on the couch. "I don't know, probably just typical Gwen stuff. You know, the mental games, the bloodshed. Maybe having her turn him was a bad idea."

Elizabeth raised an eyebrow. "You mean what I said from the beginning? Had I known what you two were doing—"

"Yes, I know. We should have asked your opinion."

"Because clearly I am the smartest in the group. I'm still alive, after all."

She had a point. She survived all these centuries not because of her strength but because she could outwit all the demons combined. Granted, she was still very strong; she usually didn't have to fight much and worked through everything with her quick thinking. The only other person as clever as her was Gwen, but she liked games the most. Even though she liked having fun, she hadn't slipped up yet.

"Do you think he will be able to resist her? I mean, he can't stand any blood other than hers. The thirst will get the better of him one of these days."

Elizabeth didn't say anything but finished drying her hair with her towel. They sat there in silence as they waited for Collin to step out of the bath. Erik had a feeling he wouldn't be long, as normally he always took a quick shower.

Moments later Erik found he was right, and he heard the water stop. A few minutes later, Collin stepped out with his towel wrapped around his waist.

"Sorry, I forgot to grab clothes," he mumbled as he hurried off to his room. After he changed, he stepped back out of his room and took a seat.

"Well then, what should we do first?"

Erik leaned forward. "Well, first thing is first. Tell us what Gwen said. We need you to be honest with us so we can get an idea of what game she's trying to play. We won't judge you for anything you did, but we need to know everything if we're going to stop them. Believe us, we have seen her cruelty. It's easy to fall into her traps."

Collin's eyes moved between him and Elizabeth. He played with his hands for a moment and rocked back and forth. Finally he nodded. "I went to their hotel, and Gwen and James were there. Gwen offered me her blood, and I took it. I wanted to resist, but the urge was too much."

Erik nodded. "That is only natural. You can't stomach anything else."

Collin peered down at his hands. "I tried to leave, but then she took my blood and said that next time she didn't want my blood but wanted information about you two. I, of course, didn't give her any then, but I fear that if the urge becomes too strong…"

Erik let out a breath. He figured it would come down to this. Gwen was going to try to use him against them. That was typical for her, but he still couldn't believe it.

Elizabeth stood up. "Well then, I guess we'll give her information."

Both Collin and Erik stared at her. Erik was the first to speak. "Are you crazy? We can't give her information. We can't let her have any advantage."

Elizabeth rolled her eyes. "Not real information. See, this is why you're lucky to have me around. We give her information just like they did to us in London—we set them up and take the ones that are here down, or at least one or two."

It wasn't a bad plan, but if he knew demons, they weren't the most trusting folk. They couldn't even trust each other, not to mention they were such liars that they would expect everyone around them to lie as well.

"You think they will buy it though? That he would actually leak information in exchange for blood?" Erik asked.

Elizabeth shrugged. "Worth a shot. Either way we would be ready."

"She will buy it," Collin said. "She thinks I would crack in exchange for her blood."

Erik watched as Collin sat there lost in his thoughts. "What makes you say that?"

"Because she isn't talking to the others about me. She thinks she can control me. Gwen made James leave the room when I asked for blood. He didn't agree with what she was doing," Collin explained. "She is making decisions on her own because she thinks I'm wrapped around her little finger."

Erik pondered the information. That meant there was turmoil in their relationship still when it came to Collin. Gwen wasn't using her head. This could be their chance. She might stumble again, and their entire ivory tower would come crashing down once and for all.

They would make this work—they had to.

"So this could be our break then to take Gwen down once and for all." Elizabeth grinned. "I like the sound of that."

"We have to be careful though," Erik added. "There are at least four of them here, isn't that correct Collin?"

He nodded. "Yes, I can sense four of them. Gwen, James, that large scary one from London, and one other."

Erik leaned against the table. "So we still don't know where the fifth is, but either way we're outnumbered. We'll have to corner Gwen or one of the others and destroy them."

Elizabeth shook her head. "No, it will be Gwen. She is the strongest. We need to take her down first, then James won't be a problem. The other three will have to join forces, and we can take them down between the three of us."

Erik knew she was right, but he watched as Collin looked down at his hands, not wanting to think about the girl he once loved dead by his hands. Not to mention, she was the only source of blood for him. If they killed her, what would happen to him? If she died, he would too. But in the end, she had to die, and Collin knew the price he would have to pay. If there was something they could do, he would do it, but this was the only way. They would have to use any means necessary.

CHAPTER NINE

Gwen

Gwen stopped in front of the Bundesdruckerei with James's hand in hers. They would have to disrupt communications to the outside world for a bit and then lock all doors. Then this entire building would be theirs, and no one could stop them, not even the Gargoyles.

She knew that they had something up their sleeves. They had been quiet, other than Collin showing up to their hotel. They were pretty stealthy as well, and if it weren't for Collin, she wouldn't have detected them. But thus far, they hadn't stopped them from making any minions.

"Shall I do the honors?" James asked.

She gestured to the building. "After you, my darling."

James disappeared in a flash. He would go around back and find where the electricity and communications were connected to the building and disrupt them for what they had in store next. Gwen counted the seconds that went by in her head.

One. Two. Three. Four. Five. Six. Seven.

He appeared again. She cocked an eyebrow. "What took you so long?"

They stepped inside the building together. "Had to find the phone lines, didn't I?"

Gwen stuck out her tongue playfully as they walked up to the front desk. A woman with curly dark brown hair and a nice suit glanced up at them.

"How may I help you?"

James leaned forward on his arms with a flirtatious smile on his face. "We are here to meet with Herr Kaufman."

"What is your name?"

"James Arthur."

The receptionist picked up the phone to connect to

his office. She got a puzzled look on her face. "For some reason our phones are out. Excuse me for just a moment."

James nodded. "No problem." She left the desk and them behind. James turned to Gwen and raised an eyebrow. "Are you ready?"

"Ready as I'll ever be." Gwen turned to the handful of security guards that stood in front of a few of the doors. In an instant the two of them attacked and bit at their necks. They didn't even have time to scream.

Gwen grabbed the keys from one of the security guards and quickly locked the doors.

"Easy peasy." Gwen smiled as she swung the keys in her hand. "Now no one can come in or call out."

"Now for the fun part." James licked the blood off his lips as they used the scanner card they had picked up from the guard and opened the door.

"According to Wiki, there is about two thousand people employed here," Gwen commented.

"Well then, hope you're hungry."

Gwen smiled as her eyes turned yellow. "Don't worry, I am."

The Bundesdruckerei had changed since the last time the two of them took it over. Gwen was impressed with how high-tech it now was. Rooms in which documents and passports were made were now in clean rooms and everyone wore white. After they were through, however, many of the rooms were going to need to be cleaned as blood stained the floors.

Although they had been attacking bars and clubs, there was something different when going after a company like this. There was more screaming and more needing to track down everyone. It felt more like a horror movie in that sense, or at least that was what Gwen felt. These people were just doing their jobs, and they were going to be killed for that.

No, Gwen thought, *I will not regret this. I can't have any more regrets.*

An easy way to destroy regret was to not look the humans in the eyes as they pleaded for their life. Gwen learned that long ago. And she had learned to remind herself that these humans would die in a short amount of time anyway, or at least a short amount of time to demons. They had lived for centuries upon centuries, roaming the earth. She had to remind herself if she failed, then the rest of her days would be in hell for the rest of eternity. The time she spent on Earth would seem like a sweet afternoon parade to what was in store for her.

She had a feeling Lucifer had a special plan for her if all this failed since it would be her fault. It had been a while since he visited Earth in his temporary form. If she calculated it right, he should be due to show up and be in her hair any day now. She was not looking forward to that visit.

Gwen watched as James bit a worker's neck, his face full of glee. Gwen hadn't seen him this happy in decades. She was glad he wasn't as grumpy as he had been earlier that morning. It must have been about Collin, or partially because of him. She swore she didn't have feelings for him anymore, at least not in the way she loved James. For Collin, originally it had been something else. Now it was much more complicated, but he wasn't someone Gwen would ever leave James for. She had seen what crap he had to put up with from the others when she left—she felt guilty and appreciated the fact that he never gave up on her. Part of it was probably because of the blood bond and he couldn't function without her, but she knew the other part had to be due to his love for her.

Bodies littered the rooms and hallways now. Gwen stepped over a redheaded worker, listening for any movement. Had they killed everyone? Would their minions soon be awakening?

James glanced around as well. "I don't sense anyone else. How about you?"

Gwen shook her head. "I don't…" That was when she heard it—soft crying. Gwen put her finger to her lips and followed the noise. They walked into an office and found a woman hiding under her desk.

"Well, you found her," James said. "You can have the honors."

Gwen grabbed the woman and bit into her neck before she could plea for her life. Tossing the body aside, Gwen collapsed into the woman's chair.

James raised an eyebrow. "That much blood and you're tired? That isn't like you."

"I'm just tired of this war."

"Well, whose fault is that?"

She let out a brief laugh. "Fair point. I just don't want to deal with any of this anymore. The humans are always changing things and moving forward, and we'll always be the same. It seems strange, doesn't it? Why don't we change?"

James leaned against the desk in front of her.

"Because we are different and aren't fickle. We don't

care about change, and time is meaningless." James grabbed her hand and kissed it. "We don't grow tired of each other either. Put two humans together and they might kill each other eventually, after they get bored of their company that is."

Gwen laughed. "Yes, that is one of the ways we differ. Then there is the whole condemned to hell part."

"Not if we destroy the Gargoyles. Not if we finally bring terror upon this earth. Then there will be no hell waiting for us." James let go of her hand and paced to the window, staring out at the streets below. "What did Darrell and you talk about earlier?"

Gwen felt her heart skip a beat. "Darrell? What do you mean?"

"Before you came into the meeting, Darrell pulled you aside. What did he ask you?"

She debated telling him the truth. "He just asked if we actually got to our hotel room last night. You know how he gets curious." She decided to lie even though she knew he wouldn't believe it.

James shook his head. "That's not what he asked. It was about me, wasn't it?"

Gwen hesitated. "Yes, it was. He was wondering if something was wrong."

He turned to face her. "And what did you say?"

"I said I didn't know." She watched as he held his gaze, then looked away. "What is bothering you?"

James took in a deep breath and let it out slowly. "It's nothing."

She grabbed him by the wrist before he could turn back to look outside. "Tell me what is going on, James. You have never given me the cold shoulder. What are you thinking?"

His eyes were cold as they looked at her. They gave her the shivers, but she didn't back down. She didn't let him intimidate her like that.

"I'm not mad at you if that is what you're thinking. I know you're back and everything, I am just worried about bringing the Gargoyles down."

"Worried? Worried how?" Gwen asked.

"I am afraid if we have another screwup, they could win and we'll be sent to hell."

"You mean you're afraid I'll screw up again."

"I didn't say that." He paused. "But it does worry me. I didn't see it coming, Gwen, then all of a sudden you left. I don't know what to look for. I don't get how you just cracked and left."

She shook her head. "I'm not going to leave you

again."

"You say that, but how do I know you aren't lying?" His voice started to rise. "How do I know you won't run off with your hybrid?"

Gwen didn't say anything. She knew he was right in asking that—he was right in not trusting her, but she knew in her heart she could never leave James again. Collin was behind her, and all she wanted to do was destroy his soul. She wanted to make him realize he should have left her alone.

The bodies around them started to stir. They had completed their mission, and now they could keep moving forward.

James kissed her cheek. "I love you, Gwen. Nothing will change that. I just don't know how far I can trust you to follow through with what you say." He looked down at the minions. "But first things first, we need to get these minions ready for the next step of the battle."

She nodded, wiping away the tears that had formed in her eye. Nothing hurt more than the loss of trust from a loved one, even if he still loved her. She didn't let him see the tears as they prepared for the final part in their mission.

CHAPTER TEN

Collin

Collin fidgeted with his sleeve as he stared at the door in front of him. She was in there. He knew that. He was given the information to tell her and knew everything he needed to do. The problem was he feared something would go wrong. He feared she would get the information she wasn't supposed to know out of him. He feared her blood would consume his soul and the Gargoyles plan would fail.

Taking a deep breath, he focused. He had to make it look like a mental struggle and as if he wasn't going to give her certain information. That information, of course, would be a trap. Only then would they be able to take the demons down.

He knocked on the door. Gwen opened it, a little smug as if she had won a bet. She wore a black dress that hugged her curves tightly. The sleeves were made of black lace, and the neckline was low. He stared at her bare neck, the thirst as strong as it was the moment he'd turned her—a thirst that was never quenched.

She leaned against the doorway. "So you decided to bring me some information then?"

He nodded slowly as she pulled him inside. James was leaning against the back of the couch.

"Well then, tell us what that is." Gwen's eyes flashed yellow as if excited. "Tell us the secrets the Gargoyles have."

He glanced at James, who kept a steady eye on him, then back to Gwen. "They are planning to go to the ministry in the morning. Explain the situation to them about you and your minions. They are going to tell them everything about the war."

She laughed. "And they expect the ministry to believe them? They expect humans to be able to do something about the war?"

Collin shrugged. "It's what they told me." He realized then that they didn't know that the ministry had been under Gargoyle control for decades now. Elizabeth was right.

James straightened up. "Where do they think you are right now?"

Collin swallowed. "Excuse me?"

"Right now. Where did you tell them you were? I presume they noticed you left. They aren't stupid."

"They know I come to Gwen. They know I need blood," Collin answered, hoping that would satisfy him.

"So you're telling us what they want you to tell us." James stepped closer and glanced to Gwen. "So the information you're giving us is what they want us to know."

"No, they think I come for blood and give my own blood in return. They don't think I am giving you information. They trust that I wouldn't."

James held his gaze a second longer, then turned to Gwen. "Guinevere, my love, you don't actually believe him, do you?"

She bit her lip. "There is always a way we could find out. Come with us to dinner tonight, then if I am satisfied you're telling the truth, I'll give you my blood."

Collin started to say something but bit his tongue, knowing she would only find it fun to taunt him even more. Unfortunately, she saw his hesitation.

She giggled. "You don't want to wait for blood, do you?"

He just stared at her. She grabbed him and pulled him close. Moving her hair out of the way, she whispered into his ear. "Go ahead then. Take some now."

Collin knew James was hating every moment of this, and to be fair, so was he. He hated this need he had in his heart—how it controlled him so. But it was the only way to play along. Slowly he bit into her neck, letting the blood consume him. Gwen just laughed.

He felt as if he couldn't stop. The life and power that flowed through his body was unlike anything he ever felt before. The feeling didn't fade with time; it stayed the same. It never faded.

Something pulled him back, and he turned to find James's hand around his wrist. "That's enough. You had your fun."

Collin didn't know if he was talking to him or Gwen.

Gwen smiled as she wiped the blood off her neck. "James, calm down. You are scaring the poor boy." She placed her bloody fingers on his lips. "You need to learn to share."

James eyed her as she went into the bathroom to wash up. "If it were up to me, he would be drowning in a pool of his own blood right now."

"But it's not up to you, so behave yourself," she said from the bathroom. A moment later she stepped back into the main area. "Let's go have some fun now."

Collin followed Gwen and James out of the hotel and down the streets of Berlin. He wanted to run far away from them. He didn't know where they were taking him, nor did he know what he would be up against. He had his blood and didn't need her anymore, but he knew it would be better to stay. He had to seem confused and in need of blood even though he truly didn't need it. He had to act desperate.

They walked for about fifteen minutes and came upon a small bar. The inside was dark with the quiet sound of a piano coming from the small stage that was in the back. Collin could sense two more demons in the area. He spun around to find them between him and the door.

"Well, what do we have here?" The larger one snickered. Collin remembered him from London. His name was Jürgen, he believed. "Looks like someone got lost."

"He's with us," Gwen chimed in. "And you aren't allowed to touch him."

"Is that so?" Jürgen glanced at James. "And you're just going to put up with this, James?"

"We'll see how the night goes," James said as he took a seat at the bar with Gwen.

Jürgen grunted as he joined him.

The last demon still stood between Collin and the door. He looked innocent, at least more innocent than the other three. He held out his hand. "Hi, my name is Darrell. It's a pleasure finally meeting you."

Collin stared at his hand for a moment, then shook it. "Okay."

"I can't believe Gwen left James for you. You are such a pip-squeak compared to him. He could crush you in an instant." The cheerfulness never left his face. "I'm surprised he hasn't killed you already."

"He has. That's why I'm in the state that I am in," Collin answered.

"And you have a sense of humor. That's great." Darrell gestured to the bar. "Let's take a seat. The show is just about to begin."

Collin followed him, taking a seat next to Gwen. He didn't know what Darrell meant by *show*, but he had a feeling he wouldn't like it.

Gwen nudged James and nodded toward the piano. "Please, it's been so long since you've played."

James sighed. "I can never say no to you, can I?"

She smiled as they stood up and headed toward the piano. Darrell moved over next to Collin. "They make such great partners."

Jürgen shook his head. "I can't believe they're doing this."

James made the pianist move and took a seat at the piano. People turned their attention to him as he began to play. Collin recognized the song, the *Kiss of Fire*. Gwen sat down next to him on the piano bench.

Gwen began singing in Spanish. Collin didn't know what exactly she was saying, but it sounded beautiful.

"She knows Spanish?" Collin questioned Darrell.

"We have been alive for thousands of years. We know every language ever spoken on this earth."

That made sense to Collin. Collin turned back to watch as James started singing.

Jürgen got up and headed out the back. Collin wondered if it was because he was fed up with their nonsense or if he had something else he was doing. It wasn't his place to ask, not to mention he felt very out of place.

Gwen and James sang in unison what Collin figured was the chorus. The song went on, and suddenly both their eyes flashed yellow. Collin noticed the people around him start shifting in their chairs. They all noticed and didn't understand what had happened. Gwen leaned in to James, their lips only centimeters apart as they spoke the last words of the song.

Gwen kissed him at the moment the lights turned off. Collin heard the screams of the people around him. There was nothing he could do; it happened all so fast. He smelled it, the blood. He put his hand over his mouth, trying not to vomit. It was heavy in the air; he had never been so close to it. Not that much anyway.

The lights turned back on, and every single person around him lay on the floor in a pool of their own blood. Gwen stood above the bodies, licking her lips. "Well, this went well. I half expected you to try to stop us, Collin."

He started shaking his head. "What…? What did you…?"

She stepped toward him. "I killed them, Collin,

letting their bodies be hosts for our minions. We are building an army, you know. Question is, are you setting us up?"

"What? Why would I lie?"

"The information you gave us, is it real? Or are you doing what the Gargoyles ordered you to do?"

"I already said, that is all they told me," Collin said.

Gwen glanced over toward the entrance. A woman came into the bar, seeing all the bodies on the ground. She screamed. Gwen didn't give her a chance to run away, rushing to her and placing her hand over her mouth. "Shh, it's okay. They aren't dead; they are just sleeping. Isn't that right, Collin?"

Collin stayed silent, watching as the woman in Gwen's arms struggled and tried to get away.

"I can make you fall asleep too, but really it's up to Collin here." Her eyes darted to his. "Should she live, Collin? Or should she die?"

"What are you doing?"

"It's that simple. Either you kill her completely, or I let her go. Keep in mind, if I let her go, she will alert more people and I'll have to deal with them as well. Doesn't look pretty either way." Gwen slowly sliced her nail against the woman's throat. "She does smell delicious though, don't you think?"

The blood dripped down the woman's neck, and Collin could feel his eyes change. He shook his head. "Stop it! I can't stomach a human's blood!"

"I could kill her for you, Collin, just tell me the truth. What are the Gargoyles planning? And you have to be pretty convincing."

Collin stared at her and the woman she held. There was no hope for the woman, but he knew he couldn't kill her. And this would make his confession even more convincing. Gwen was actually doing him a favor. "They… They are planning to corner you. They aren't going to the ministry to talk to them. They are going to wait for you."

Gwen smiled. "There's a good boy." She sank her fangs into the woman she held, draining her of all her blood. Collin looked away, trying not to think about joining her. He hated these urges; he hated the way she used him. He hated her.

Shoving past Gwen, he ran out of the bar.

CHAPTER ELEVEN

James

James laughed as he watched Collin run off. He thought him such a human, being dramatic with everything going on. People were going to die; he just needed to accept that. They were such fragile creatures. They didn't understand the true meaning of power. They didn't understand the entire universe that was out there and how they were nothing compared to the beings of Heaven and hell. They only knew what they could see of the Earth around them.

James debated going after him and tying him down to watch them torture even more humans. Eventually he would crack. They always did. It was why they weren't allowed to make more minions. Collin was the exception, and James had to admit he did come in handy, as they were able to take down one Gargoyle. Hugo, James believed his name was. If he recalled correctly, the Gargoyle had given him troubles during the Golden Age of Piracy. He could have extended the times the pirates ruled the seas if it weren't for him. It was good riddance that they had finally destroyed him.

Gwen approached him with a smug look on her face. She got what she wanted out of him finally. James didn't think she would be able to go through with mentally torturing him, but she did it. Or at least it seemed like that was what she wanted. Perhaps she really was back to normal. He still had his suspicions, however.

"Well then." Gwen grabbed the glass of wine that still was on the bar where she sat earlier. "How shall we go about playing this game?"

"They thought they could set us up?" Jürgen grinned. "They think they can get the German government to trust them? And be able to corner us? We have woven a deep web in this area. There is no way they can take this place back."

"I agree. We have the home advantage. We have thousands of minions working for us already. We can't lose." Gwen drank the last of the wine. "We'll take them down once and for all. All two of them are here, by the smell on Collin's clothes."

"Don't get ahead of yourself, Gwen. Remember what happened last time you said that," Jürgen grumbled.

"I won't betray Lucifer. I learned my lesson the first time. I am on board for destroying the last Gargoyles. This needs to end here and now."

"Again, that's what you said the first time."

Gwen sighed.

James knew Jürgen wasn't going to let up. He wrapped his arms around Gwen and kissed the side of her head. "Gwen has been a good girl and killed all the people in the Bundesdruckerei. I didn't see any regret in her eyes, so you have nothing to worry about. Besides, I'm keeping an ever closer eye on her. So chill, all right?"

Jürgen grunted but didn't say a word. If James was honest, he expected Jürgen to make a jab at how James would do anything Gwen said. Perhaps he did see that James wasn't going to let anything happen this time. They had too much to lose.

Gwen bit her lip. "I wonder how much the Gargoyles actually planned out. What if he was acting like he was giving in and they had two fake plans to give us?"

Jürgen nodded. "She has a point, unfortunately."

"So if they want us to think they are going to go to the ministry, then where do you think they are actually going to go?" James asked. He pondered that thought, as it seemed like it would be something they would do.

Gwen shrugged. "I can't honestly think of anything else they would do. I mean, it's apparent that we have control of this city. Do they not realize how many minions we have collected? We are in the thousands. There is no way they could destroy them all without hysteria. They have not won."

James nodded. "You are right. No matter what they try, they have lost this country. But that doesn't mean they won't try to take the four of us out."

Darrell sighed. "He has a point. They probably aren't aiming to help countries anymore but just to destroy us. Honestly it's what they should have always done, but they always got distracted by helping humans. It's sad, really."

"We'll call upon all our minions to help. There is no way they would be able to get past all of them to get to us. Then, once we have them surrounded, we'll tear out their hearts." Jürgen grinned at the idea of holding a Gargoyle heart in his hand.

James had to agree, it was one of the best feelings in all the world.

"But it still doesn't make sense," Gwen added. "What was their plan for Collin telling us what he said?"

James shrugged. "It doesn't matter, Gwen sweetie. There is no way they can win."

Gwen bit at her nails. "Elizabeth is still with them. She is smart and knows how to plan without using brute force. She will be ready for us. They have something in mind. I can feel it."

Darrell placed his hand on Gwen's shoulder. "Cheer up. We outnumber them—it will be fine. There should be nothing to worry about, okay? We'll attack the House of Parliament, turn them all into minions, and be on our merry way to Russia where Seth is waiting."

"Nice and chilly this time of year." Gwen laughed. "Been a while since I've enjoyed those icy nights."

James pulled her close. "Don't worry. I'll keep you

warm."

Jürgen grunted. "Let's finish planning here. They expect to corner us in the morning, and we'll show them what is really in store for them."

"Unless Collin tells them otherwise," Gwen explained. "He saw what we did here. They know we made our armies."

"So question is, why would they risk it?" James finished. "I'm starting to see your concern, Gwen. Perhaps we really should stop and think about this."

Gwen nodded. "There are three of them and four of us. We have minions; they do not. They think the German government is going to listen? They think they will understand? No, there has to be something we don't see."

"They believed you in London," Jürgen added. "They fell into our trap and thought they would win. They just could be foolish. Perhaps they are worn out. I know I would be, having to deal with your tactics."

Gwen grinned, and James recalled all the things they had done to the Gargoyles over the centuries. It was a blast to say the least. When they were gone, he would miss their favorite playthings.

"Then what should we do?" Darrell asked.

"We could activate their trap, see what they are truly hiding. Bring all our minions and surround them. They could be underestimating our power here," Gwen said. "Take down the German government and be finished."

"You really think we should risk it?" Jürgen stared at James.

James pondered the thought. Yes, it was all too easy, but so was last time. They set Gwen up, and they believed her. They could trust Collin not to say anything about tomorrow and plan on us coming without backup. They would be foolish though, and being this close to the end of the war, James thought they would have learned by now. But there was one thing they had that they could use against them. Collin.

"Gwen, what if Collin attacks you?" James asked.

She raised an eyebrow. "Excuse me?"

"When it comes down to it, will you be able to kill him?"

She placed her hand on his cheek and stared into his eyes. "I already told you, yes. Without a blink of an eye, I'll kill him when his use to me is up."

James watched as Jürgen stared at her for a moment, then turned back to him. "Then after these minions awaken, we should prepare."

James nodded. "Right. And perhaps tomorrow will be the last day we'll have to ever fight."

CHAPTER TWELVE

Erik

Erik checked the clock. It was almost two in the morning, and Collin wasn't back yet. Pacing back and forth in the room, Erik waited. Collin was nowhere to be seen. He should have had enough time with Gwen.

"Calm down. You're starting to make me worry." Elizabeth lay on the couch, staring up at the ceiling.

"He should have been back by now." Erik glanced at the clock again. Not even a minute had passed.

Elizabeth sighed. "He's probably calming himself down after having to face Gwen. I know I would need a couple of hours to cool down."

"We have a plan to follow. He needs to get here soon." Erik stopped and rubbed his face with his rough hands. "This is our only chance. We need to take out as many minions as we can. We gathered many during the day, but who knows how many more they have made."

"And Collin knows that. Just let him walk it off. You know how she can get under your skin," Elizabeth said. "Or do I have to remind you of the times she drained your blood over and over again? Slicing your heart just enough where you still lived?"

Erik closed his eyes. "No, you don't need to remind me."

"And yet you still let her in," she whispered.

"And I was right to. If it weren't for her and James's blood bond, she could have helped us."

"I can't believe you let her come near us."

"We needed her to turn Collin. Besides, something made her want to repent." Erik bit at his nail. "It made me curious what exactly was going through her mind."

And he truly meant that. It made no sense after everything she had done for her to try to be redeemed.

She was the worst of them all. Had it all been a front? Did she want to appear as if nothing was wrong and she was a bad guy so she could destroy their chance of opening up the gates of hell? Erik knew it wasn't something to rely on, but it made him think—if she was capable of remorse, if all the fallen Angels were, why couldn't they be forgiven like humans who turned their back on God could? It was something that always bothered him, but he never spoke it out loud. He didn't want to seem he was questioning God.

"Well, she can't repent, Erik. There is nothing for her to gain. Besides, even if she really did want to help, you have no reason to let her. We should have just killed her."

Erik shook his head. "We couldn't. We needed her to change Collin."

"After that then. You should have killed her."

He let out a sigh. They had been over this a thousand times, but Elizabeth couldn't stop pestering him about it. He couldn't blame her as the stakes were high and their nerves were high. "I couldn't do that."

She waved her arms up. "Oh right. The blood pact. You were stupid enough to do that. Gwen could have killed us with that. None of us could touch her without dying. She could have killed me, then you."

"I knew she wouldn't."

Elizabeth turned her head to face him. "How?"

"Because that would be too easy. She would never do something so easy. It wouldn't be fun."

She let out a breath. "Sadly, I know you're right. I'll give you that one, but you were still foolish to agree to a blood pact."

He let out a breath. "Don't worry. I won't ever do it again."

"Good, I might have to kill you if you think about trying that ever again."

Erik laughed as he heard the hotel door open. Collin stood in the entry, eyes dark and lips in a frown. His hair was messed up, and he had drops of blood splattered on his shirt. It was just like the other night, but this time it was worse—this time he appeared white like a ghost.

"Collin, are you…?"

"It's done. They know you want to set them up tomorrow. They will bring their minions and we'll take them all down," he said as he headed toward his room.

Erik grabbed his wrist. "Wait, what happened? What took you so long?"

Collin didn't face him. "They took me to a bar, and they slaughtered everyone there. Gwen tried to get me to kill an innocent person, or I could tell them the truth of what you're doing tomorrow. I told them what you wanted me to tell them, and they bought it. Then she killed the woman, and I ran out. I wandered the streets for hours trying to get the stench of blood out of my lungs." Collin turned to face Erik, his eyes a demonic yellow. "Now, can I go change?"

Erik let go of Collin's wrist and watched as his eyes changed back to normal. Collin went into his room and closed the door. Erik felt bad for making him say all that out loud. But he had to know what happened—secrets would get them nowhere.

"Told you he was just cooling off after something Gwen did." Elizabeth still hadn't moved from the couch. Usually by now she would be up pacing around. Her legs must have been tired, not that they got tired that easily.

"Fine, you win that bet." He glanced back at the closed door. "I just worry."

She straightened up. "He will be fine."

"You sure about that?"

"Out of anyone, yes. I think he will be able to handle

this. Especially if everything goes according to plan."

"That's the problem though," Erik said. "Nothing ever goes according to plan."

Elizabeth chuckled as she stood up. "Isn't that a fact? But we should go out and find minions if we want to counter their defenses."

Erik nodded. "You are right. We need to hurry now more than ever." He knocked on Collin's door. "Collin, I know you're stressed, but we need you."

Collin was the one who could sense where minions were since they smelled of death, according to him. Collin could point them out, and Erik and Elizabeth could destroy them before they even became a problem. At first Collin helped dispose of them, but the larger the number became and seeing the families who had no idea that their family member was now possessed by a demon, he started to have second thoughts. It was just easier for him if he pointed them out.

Erik waited for Collin to let him in or answer him, but there was no sound. Erik slowly opened the door to find Collin sitting on his bed, facing the window.

"Collin?"

He shook his head. "I can't keep doing this. I can't keep seeing so much blood. It was bad enough, destroying minions with Hugo for all that time, and the nightmares… Now I can't sleep, and I just keep seeing more and more blood. It's as if I'm in a dream that will never end. I don't know what to do, Erik. I know this is for the good of the world—for good itself—but I don't think I can take much more of it."

Erik took a seat next to him. He realized perhaps he and Elizabeth were wrong. Or perhaps it was the fact that he wasn't corrupt and still had good in his heart was the reason he was suffering so much. Erik knew he wouldn't betray them, but to see him suffering with such a dilemma made Erik begin to regret his decision on forcing Gwen to turn him fully.

"Nothing about this war has been easy. Elizabeth and I have seen countless friends die because of the demons."

"But they just go back to Heaven, right? Is that really much to lose?"

Erik opened his mouth to answer but closed it again. He had a point—they were eternal beings and these bodies weren't their own. Even if his friends had died, he would see them in Heaven—but that didn't mean it wasn't painful to watch how they were tortured and played with by the demons. And with every one of them gone, it meant the demons were closer to winning the war—the war that would determine the fate of the human race.

"Collin… I know it's hard, but think about how many humans you're saving. If the demons win, then that means Lucifer will take over this world. Humans will only know limitless suffering and will never accept God into their hearts. With that, the downfall of all humans will happen and this entire world will be the new hell."

Collin grabbed his head. "You think I don't realize that? You don't think I know what countless things the demons will do to everyone if they win? But that is the problem! All that pressure is on my head now!"

Erik knew that feeling all too well. "It isn't just on your shoulders. Everything is in God's hands. You understand that, right?"

"Then why does it feel so hard? If he wanted us to win, why couldn't he make it easy? It's not like you lot have anything to prove."

"That's where you're wrong." Erik sighed. He hated thinking about the history of Heaven and how the war began. "All demons come from Heaven. They were once Angels or like us. So we are equally matched. The reason God doesn't give us an upper hand is so he can make sure we are faithful to him because we want to be instead of being faithful because we want power. Lucifer promised the others power and freedom to do what they wished. He, however, twists words and, well, you have seen the Twelve. They are powerful but not in the way that Lucifer promised."

Collin didn't say anything for a moment. He seemed to be gathering everything Erik had said and putting it together. The details of the war weren't something any of them liked talking about to humans, mainly because it would just scare them that something so much larger was going on, but it was time that Collin really understood what he was up against.

He slowly nodded. "I understand now. It's not about me—it's not about what I have witnessed. I need to keep pressing forward so that humanity as a whole can survive. Those who suffer in front of me will be met by God in Heaven."

Erik patted his back. "Exactly. So don't fret it. We need to go out there and decrease the number of minions. So grab your sword and let's go."

"Yeah. Right."

CHAPTER THIRTEEN

Gwen

Gwen bit at her nails. What were they planning? She had a feeling there was something she was missing, but she couldn't quite figure out what that was. She sipped on her wine as she stared out at the city street. All she wore was a white silk robe as she waited for James to get out of the shower. Granted, she thought about joining him, but this puzzle still eluded her.

Collin was definitely not going to give information

for blood yet, that was for certain. She would have to remedy that with some nice torture or really trick him. She wondered if she could get information by convincing him she had a guilty conscious still and that all this was a ruse. She pushed that idea away, however, as it would just leave Jürgen and Seth suspicious. That was the last thing she needed.

But she did need to figure this out before it was too late—she needed to know what the Gargoyles were up to.

If it was Erik and Hugo, then she wouldn't worry like this. They weren't the brightest Gargoyles in the bunch, but they had stayed alive, mainly because of her. She liked to torture them and play games, which ultimately led to them escaping. She had gotten in trouble more than once for such things, but it was most definitely worth it. She loved to see their troubled faces.

But Elizabeth was different. She hated dealing with that bitch. Elizabeth was always one step ahead of her, and Gwen wanted more than anything to take her down. There wasn't time for games anymore, and Gwen would kill her quick and easy herself. Then she would be the last one laughing. Gwen recalled all the times she had almost lost her life to Elizabeth. There were quite a few close calls, and if it weren't for James and Darrell, she would be in hell right now. So she couldn't let her guard down—not when Elizabeth was still alive.

Gwen knew that the only reason the demons had been so successful in London was because she didn't show up until the end and because she herself was a wildcard, and they used that to their advantage. And Erik was stupid enough to perform a blood deal with James. If Elizabeth had shown up any sooner, things would have gone a bit differently, mainly she would probably be dead. It had been close when she had shown up in the apartment.

She took a sip of her wine and let out a sigh. She could feel how close they were getting. It was only a matter of time until they unlocked the doors to hell. Or fail and she would face an eternal punishment. Either way, things were going to change for better or worse.

Gwen heard the shower turn off, and she watched as James stepped out of the bathroom with just a towel around his waist. She raised an eyebrow.

"What? Are you trying to be modest now?"

He nodded toward the windows. "The shades are open. I wouldn't want you to get jealous if some woman on the sidewalk decides to come up here and knock on my door."

Gwen laughed. "That happened only twice."

"Yeah, and you killed them both, didn't you?"

Gwen smiled. That she did. Although James flirted quite often, she didn't like being interrupted on her own turf or what she considered to be her turf. Anywhere her bed was she called home since they never really had a home. Not since Heaven anyway.

James took a seat next to her and kissed her hair. "What are you thinking about out here all by your lonesome?"

She shrugged. "Nothing, really. I am just wondering what the Gargoyles have planned. Elizabeth is clever, and I don't trust her."

"Honey, we don't trust any of them in the first place. That is why we are at war."

She snickered. "Yeah, I know. But you know what I mean. She'd almost killed us before. Collin knows we've made a lot of minions and severely outnumber them. Even if they are mindless minions and easy to kill for them, there gets to be a point where you can't move, which is the plan."

"Perhaps they don't think we have that many minions —perhaps they think we have a lot less than the thousands that we do."

James made a fair point. Collin had only seen them create a couple hundred when really it was many more. If Gwen had her way, the entire country would be turned, then they really wouldn't have to worry. But there were only so many demons ready to possess, not to mention having to deal with that many minions would just be troublesome.

Leaning in, James kissed her on the mouth. "How about I take your mind off it?"

Gwen liked where that was going. "It has been quite a few hours since I've tasted your blood on my lips."

He grinned his cocky grin. "And I need to get you back for letting another man taste your blood."

She let out a fun yelp as he picked her up and took her into the bedroom. As he set her down on the bed, he kissed her neck and sank his fangs into her skin. Gwen let out a euphoric gasp as she felt connected to her lover —her sin—the one she left Heaven for. There was no going back because she never wanted power, which Lucifer still hadn't provided, but the love of James. In Heaven, they couldn't love each other in the way the two of them wanted to, and Lucifer promised an eternity where James and Gwen could be with each other. They didn't have to think twice.

James let go of her neck, and she spun him around and was now on top of him. She too wanted a taste of the forbidden fruit that caused their downfall. She bit into his neck, and the warm, red liquid gushed into her mouth, tasting as sweet as honey. No blood compared, not even Collin's. It was why she didn't care to drink from him—not when she could use information he gave to bring down the Gargoyles. All she needed was James's blood.

She could stay like this forever and forget about the Gargoyles and the rest of the Twelve, but that would cause more harm than good. The Twelve would come after them, and then they would be eternally damned, not that they weren't already. It would just be a faster process. No, they had to finish this war, and then they could do whatever they wanted. They could stay in a room like this until the sun expanded and devoured the Earth. Gwen liked the sound of that.

Gwen backed away, blood dripping down her chin and onto James's bare chest. She licked it off him as she stared at him straight in the eyes.

"Ah." James smirked. "It's going to be one of those nights."

She giggled as he flipped on top of her and began to kiss her deeply.

Gwen woke to find that it was still dark out. She was surprised, as she swore it was late in the night when she and James had finally stopped ravaging each other. Standing up, she wrapped the blanket she had slept with around her naked, blood-encrusted body and stared out at the moon. It was full and beautiful—more beautiful than she had seen in quite some time.

This beauty, she wondered, *would it be destroyed by Lucifer?* He grew jealous of anything that shone brighter and more wondrous than him and would make it turn into dust. She didn't want to see the destruction of the moon and stars and a lot of the earth's nature. It would be a waste of something so grand. The humans were already destroying all that they could. Would Lucifer be even worse, or will he side with the animals and plants and wipe out the humans altogether?

Gwen shook her head. No, they needed the humans. She knew that. It was how they sustained these bodies and were able to walk on Earth. But if the gates of hell were opened, then did that mean they wouldn't have to worry about such things anymore? She and James would still enjoy each other's blood, but the idea of not having to feed on a human excited her. She would be free of the chain that drove her to insanity. Granted, she would be the one helping destroy it all, but at least after a while it would be over.

"I can't believe after all that, your mind is still racing."

Gwen turned and found James sitting up in bed, watching her. She smiled and climbed back into bed next to him. He wrapped his arm around her and stroked her hair.

"It's not just tomorrow. I keep thinking about what's going to happen when those gates open, and my mind starts to wander."

"Oh? How so?"

"I mean, will he destroy all the humans? Will he destroy this entire planet? Or will he keep it the same and slowly corrupt it so that no human will ever taste Heaven?"

James shrugged. "What does it matter? We'll be given the freedom and power that was promised. I don't really care what he does with the place. We have had our fun, and I just want the rest of eternity to be with you."

She snuggled up against him. His skin was warm and felt soothing to her body.

"I guess you're right. I shouldn't worry."

"I'm right? Wait, say that again. I love hearing you say that."

She laughed. "You're right. This once, I mean. It's a rare occasion."

"For admitting I am right, yes. As for me being right, I am always right."

"In your dreams."

"Speaking of dreams." He yawned. "Let's get some rest. We do have a big day tomorrow, after all."

She knew he was right and leaned her head against his chest. While hearing his soothing heartbeat, she fell fast asleep.

CHAPTER
FOURTEEN

Collin

Collin was tired. It wasn't like a normal tired where he just wanted to sleep but more of a feeling in his soul. He had technically been helping the Gargoyles for over five years, which was beginning to feel like an eternity. He wanted more than anything to be done with this war and couldn't imagine what the Gargoyles were feeling. They had been on Earth, fighting in this war for two thousand years, and in Heaven for even longer. Collin couldn't imagine what it would be like to live that long. Would the years go by quickly after a hundred years? A thousand? Would they feel the same and it seem like an eternity? All he knew, it wasn't something he ever wanted to experience.

Taking a deep breath, Collin tried to sense where the minions were. There were many turned in the past few days. They wouldn't be able to destroy them all, but they could dwindle a lot of their numbers. Lucky for them, they seemed to be out, prowling the streets for their next victim. The local news channels had commented that there was an increase in physical assaults in Berlin, but that was because of all the minions.

Some minions, however, resumed the human lives that their original souls once lived. They tried to act like nothing was wrong to throw the Gargoyles off their track. Those were the ones that Collin couldn't kill—it didn't feel right. If they finished cleaning up the streets for the night, Erik and Elizabeth would deal with those. He just couldn't stomach it. Erik and Elizabeth wiped the memories of any family members, made up an explanation of what happened to the person, and then disposed of the bodies.

There were just so many this time. In London, there weren't that many of them, but this time it was as if they were building a large army. That made sense to Collin since it was apparent that they were going to try to attack the Parliament.

"So, where do you sense them?" Erik asked.

Collin took another deep breath and pointed. "That way. I believe that is Alexanderplatz, if I remember my map right."

Erik nodded. "That is indeed the area. How many do you sense?"

Collin closed his eyes and focused. There was so much blood—so much foul stench. "I'm not sure. It seems like quite a few. They must have turned a lot of people during the day, on top of those at the bar."

Elizabeth folded her arms. "Such animals. They haven't turned this many people in years. They really are planning for the end, aren't they?"

Erik nodded. "It seems so. Well, this time we have a plan—this time we'll destroy any chance they had in growing an army. They won't know what hit them tomorrow. Good thing we made extra Holy water. Once that is in the air surrounding us, the demons won't be able to smell the bloodshed."

"What exactly is the plan for tomorrow?" Collin asked. "I mean, I know you didn't give me the details in case Gwen tried to get them out of me, but it would help to know now."

Elizabeth and Erik exchanged glances. Elizabeth was the one to answer his question. "We are going to blow up the building."

Collin's eyes widened. "What? But what about the people inside?"

Erik shook his head. "There won't be any humans inside. We already talked to the heads, and most agreed. The rest we used our powers on. No one will be there. The demons will show up, go inside hoping to change the head officials, and all of them including the minions will be in the blast."

"Will that kill the demons? I mean, I know it will take down a minion, but what about the Twelve?"

Erik shrugged. "It should? If they are on fire, they theoretically can burn to death. But they are pretty hardy and can heal. It will at least put them at a disadvantage, and we can wait for them to step out of the rubble and deal the final blow. If only we had the triduanum, then it would be a lot easier. I presume they have that hidden away so we can't use it against them."

Collin recalled that knife. It was called the three-day knife since it was made from the spear that pierced Jesus's side. Just like he'd risen in three days, a demon would die three days after getting stabbed with the blade. They could, however, be healed by another demon's blood. But if one had a demon cornered, it could be a great advantage. However, it seemed the demons tortured each other with it if another demon messed up. James had used it on Gwen to make her drink Collin's blood and turn him into a hybrid. Gwen had also used it on James earlier when he attacked Collin. So yeah, it seemed to him that it was more used by the demons on each other than by the Gargoyles. The Gargoyles probably didn't want to wait three days for the demons to die but killed them right away to make sure the deed was done.

"Perhaps I can get Gwen to tell me where it is, that is if they survive this blast," Collin commented as they kept walking. They weren't too far from Alexanderplatz, so it didn't make sense to take the U-Bahn.

"If there is a need, but I doubt you will need to. Our plan will bring them down. I can feel it," Erik said.

Elizabeth nodded. "Besides, she's not going to tell

you. She's not that stupid."

Collin knew she had a point. There was no reason for Gwen to tell Collin since it wasn't anything that could hurt the Gargoyles.

They kept moving forward, and before Collin knew it, they were standing in the middle of Alexanderplatz. It was well past three in the morning, and no one was out except drunk people stumbling back to their hotel or apartment and homeless people sleeping on benches and any other place that they could find. He felt bad for them—not only were they scraping by with what they had each and every day, but they were at a higher risk of getting attacked by minions.

Collin slowly breathed and pointed. "That way. There is a large gathering of them. They are probably getting ready for whatever they think is going to happen tomorrow."

"Do you sense any of the Twelve?" Erik asked as they headed down one of the alleyways.

Collin shook his head. "No. I don't sense them around here. Gwen and James are back in their hotel, and the other two are across town. If I am correct, they are making more minions."

Erik started to pick up the pace. "Well, at least we

can get this group and there will be less to deal with tomorrow. Although I know the blast will get many of them, we should be better safe than sorry. Who knows how many they will keep posted outside."

"Right," Collin commented as they turned around a corner.

Before them was a crowd of minions, standing around as if waiting for directions. The moment they saw Collin and the others, they started growling and baring their fangs. Erik pulled out the Holy water he had and sprayed it through the air. The minions hissed, but it wasn't enough to burn them—it was just enough to block out the stench of blood.

They were on them in seconds, but they were no match for the three of them. Collin pulled out his sword and started to hack away at the creatures. One. Two. Three. The more he sliced, the more he began to lose count. How many minions had he killed over the years? He used to keep track, but after he was turned, he didn't bother. It didn't matter—he wasn't exactly human and didn't need to feel bad about this. He had seen firsthand what the demons did to these creatures when they had been human. He fully understood now that there were no souls in these bodies—they were just puppets for demons to control.

The bodies morphed into grotesque creatures which Collin wondered if he appeared the same when he was feasting on blood. He didn't remember, however, his fingers growing long and sharp and his face distorting as if it had been changing into a werewolf and stopped halfway. No, the only change that Collin had was his eyes and his fangs. He was glad it wasn't something like this—something to remind him he was just a beast that craved blood.

Minions, however, didn't exactly crave blood like he did, or it didn't seem that way. It was as if they just wanted to destroy anything that wasn't them or a demon. They slaughtered humans like a creature in a horror movie. The more he witnessed that, the less he felt bad about killing them.

A minion reached out and was able to grab his arm, its claws digging into his skin. Collin let out a yelp as he swung and sliced the creature's head off. It hit the ground in a thud and rolled away. Blood poured from the exposed neck. Even though he craved blood, it made him sick to see such a grotesque scene. He tried his best not to throw up. He could just throw up later, he told himself.

He slashed and hacked at the creatures, watching as they screeched and cried out. He was surprised no one came running to see what the commotion was. Perhaps it was for the best.

Collin had to admit that destroying a group of a hundred or so minions like this was much easier when the Twelve weren't around. He didn't have to worry about a demon waiting for the right chance to attack him when he was preoccupied. No, this was like the Super Smash Bros. Nintendo 64 level with all the polygons. They were easy to defeat if you kept swinging, but if you had to fight another character that level, then it would have been much harder.

Collin watched as a minion jumped on Erik's back and sliced at his head. Erik let out a surprised yelp and grabbed the minion and threw him to the ground, piercing his sword through the creature's face. Only a handful were left, and between Elizabeth, Erik, and Collin, they'd killed them all.

They were all breathing heavily as they peered down at the dead bodies. Blood trickled down Erik's face.

He wiped it away and groaned. "I'm sick of these things. They are so annoying. They aren't powerful but in numbers they can be quite a handful."

Collin nodded. "Yeah. I'd rather just fight the demons on their own. It would be fairer."

Elizabeth let out a laugh. "As if they ever play fair. But I think this put a good dent in their numbers. Do you sense any more, Collin?"

He focused, trying to find a scent outside the bodies that lay before him. He nodded. "Yeah, there is another large group over toward Großer Tiergarten."

Erik sighed. "Well, let's go get rid of those now."

CHAPTER
FIFTEEN

James

James stretched as he got out of bed. Today was the big day, and he felt fully charged and ready to go. If he had his way, the Gargoyles' reign would end that day and they could let Lucifer back into the world.

He knew things were never that easy, however. They kept telling themselves that this was going to be the day, when in reality, they were going to only face off and no one would die on either side. James would rather that happen than them to lose a man. If anything happened to him or Gwen, it would cause the other to perish as well, or at least be weak and easy to take down for them.

He let out a sigh. He knew the dangers of the blood bond, but it was the reason they'd left Heaven. They wanted to be with each other fully, no matter what that cost was. It was worth the weakness if it meant they could be together.

Peering over at Gwen, who was still sleeping soundly, he sighed. If their weakness, however, led to the Twelve's demise, then there would be hell to pay. Literally. Lucifer, not to mention the rest of the Twelve, would take it out on them for the rest of eternity. He didn't look forward to what torture Lucifer had in store for them. He didn't want to think about it, and the only way not to think about it was to succeed in taking down the Gargoyles.

Gwen stirred and her eyes flickered open. The moment she saw James, she smiled. It made James's heart feel warm. She truly did care for him even if she'd left for all those years. It had nothing to do with him— he had to keep telling himself that. It was because of the guilt of what they had to do in Lucifer's name. It wasn't what they'd signed up for, as they just wanted to be in each other's arms. Even James had days when he wondered if he had known the full price, would he still have joined Lucifer's army? The answer was probably yes, but some nights, when he couldn't sleep, the thought rolled around in his head.

"Good morning," Gwen whispered as she stretched. "Is today the big day?"

He kissed her on the mouth. "That it is. We should probably get cleaned up."

She let out a slow breath. "I suppose. Have the others called?"

James shook his head. "Not yet. I just got up myself."

"Well then…" She stood up and hurried off toward the bathroom. "I call dibs for using the shower first."

"And here I thought we could share." James pouted.

She smirked. "But then we would take even longer to get ready."

"Well, that's fair. I better stay out here and make sure they don't call."

She closed the bathroom door and turned on the shower. James picked up his cell and checked his messages. There was a message from Jürgen.

Call me.

James rolled his eyes. He had such a way with words. James clicked the number and called Jürgen.

He answered within two rings. "About time you woke up. You know, the rest of us don't sleep as much as the two of you."

"Yeah, well, that's because none of you have quite the same workout as Gwen and I do. Believe me, we can wear each other out."

Jürgen made a gagging sound. "Forget I said anything, and keep that stuff to yourself. When the two of you are ready, meet us at Brandenburger Tor. We'll be there in thirty, so you two better get ready fast. The minions have been instructed to start filtering in around the area, or at least the ones that aren't part of the jobs we need running."

"Right. We'll be there. Don't worry."

Jürgen hung up the phone without saying goodbye. That made James laugh a little, as Jürgen had always been like that. He was stern and got things done. Nothing was ever complicated with him. With Gwen, on the other hand, she was the complete opposite. She always made things complicated.

James stepped into the bathroom. "Looks like we need to hurry, so I'll be joining you to rinse off."

Gwen rolled her eyes as he hopped into the shower.

James checked the clock on his phone. They had arrived exactly on time. He glanced around and found Jürgen already standing under the gate. He had his arms folded in front of him, as if he had been waiting for a long time. James guessed he really hadn't. Darrell was there too, his hands in his pockets, whistling as he rocked back and forth on his heels.

He remembered when Brandenburger Tor was first built by Fredrick William II of Prussia in the late 1700s. It was where the gates of Berlin once stood. Now the city engulfed it as humans increased in numbers and each city grew in size. Heck, James remembered when Berlin was just a small town in the 1100s and became the capital of Brandenburger in the 1400s. He missed Medieval Europe and all its glory. He loved watching the church burn innocent people as if they understood what was evil and what wasn't. Most of the time, evil was right under their noses and they didn't even notice. Even some of the priests during that time were minions, although that got to be complicated when the church started adding silver to everything, not to mention all that Holy water.

James hated Holy water with a passion. It just wasn't fair. It felt like acid to them, and it was just humans that blessed the water with God's will. They shouldn't be able to make such a strong weapon against them. It was one of the few things humans had that they could use. James was glad, however, that the stories of garlic hurting vampires wasn't true. He did like Italian cuisine.

Jürgen peered over and saw them. "Wow, two days in a row you've been on time. What a crazy coincidence."

Gwen folded her arms. "What is that supposed to mean."

He gave her a look. "As if you don't know."

She stuck her tongue out at him. "Well, we are here. And on time." She glanced around. "And all these people are minions."

Jürgen nodded. "Yes. Although I must admit, I could have sworn we had more."

Now that Jürgen mentioned it, the numbers did seem to be smaller than he would have thought. Honestly, he expected at least three times more minions. Something was off.

"Maybe we didn't keep count right. Or there were more with important jobs than we realized," Gwen commented.

James glanced at her. She didn't seem like she was lying, but it was still a mystery.

Darrell shrugged. "It still should be enough. There is no way the Gargoyles will be able to fight all of them off while we are attacking them. They don't stand a chance against us."

James had to admit he was right. With all these minions, the Gargoyles would have a lot of trouble. So what if a few had gone missing? Gwen was probably right; they had lost count. There was no way that the Gargoyles could have killed so many without them knowing. They would have smelled the bloodshed.

"Well then." Gwen put her arm around James. "Shall we?"

CHAPTER SIXTEEN

Erik

Erik watched as the Twelve started toward Parliament. According to Collin, all the people around the gate and toward the Reichstag building and in the park were minions. They still had a lot of minions, way more than Erik wanted. But he did admit, they had gotten rid of quite a few.

They waited in the park, hiding, their clothes covered in salt so that the Twelve couldn't sense them. He thought about putting a barrier around the entire Reichstag, but that would only be a waste of salt. Besides, he wanted them to go inside—he wanted them to meet their doom. Or at least he wanted them to be weakened and to take out as many minions as he could.

Collin tilted his head toward him. "They seem to be falling for it. There are still a lot of minions though."

Erik nodded. "But at least they don't seem too suspicious of how many showed. Perhaps they are losing their touch. Normally with something like this, they would have noticed."

"Perhaps it's because you fill the air with salt when we attack. Even I could barely sense their blood while we were killing them."

Elizabeth smiled. "You are welcome. I thought of it within the past century. I wish I had thought of it earlier than that, but alas. Here we are."

Erik had to admit, Elizabeth was good at coming up with clever ideas. He wished more of the Gargoyles were as bright as her, himself included. Perhaps they were all too tired to think clearly, or too stressed. His main stressor was the redheaded girl who'd wrapped her arms around her lover and headed straight for the Parliament.

She appeared like a lovestruck college girl who was going on a date with her new boyfriend, not some demon who was ready to slaughter them. Erik took a deep breath and slowly let it out. She always appeared like that—carefree and ready to kill with a smile. It was strange that she had sabotaged their plan all those decades ago. Erik would have thought it a ruse if he hadn't seen it firsthand. He saw the look in her eye—regret.

That look was clearly out of her eyes now. Whatever had caused it was gone. Erik felt he was more than likely responsible for that. He didn't mind, however, as he got what he wanted, and now they knew the truth about James and Gwen. If they killed one of them, the other would be extremely weakened.

Granted, that also meant the two of them were very powerful. It explained a lot, actually, as they had won countless battles. Their weakness was also their strength. But now Gwen had another weakness, and that was Collin.

Erik wondered if she really had feelings for him or if it were some fluke. He saw her eyes and the worry she had, not to mention she'd brought him back to life because James had killed him. But the question was, did she still have feelings for him? Or did she see him as some kind of pet or even a way to get to the Gargoyles?

Collin was kind, however, and Erik was grateful for that. They had trained him for years before Gwen fully turned him, and that must have made the difference. Collin still had his humanity and didn't want to kill humans. Erik prayed that was the case, and it wasn't because it took time for him to really fall. He didn't want to see the boy suffer more than he had to.

"It looks like they are heading straight in. They really don't suspect a thing. And here I thought Gwen was smarter than this," Elizabeth commented.

Erik agreed. She must have known that Collin gave her the information they wanted him to give her. Did they really just trust that this many minions would help take them down? That numbers were better than actual tactics? Erik admitted they did have a lot of minions, and under normal circumstances, they would probably take down a Gargoyle. But that wasn't the case this time—this time they were willing to destroy the entire building to weaken them.

"Should we get closer and make sure more of those minions enter the building before detonating the bombs?" Collin asked. "I don't know about you both, but I want to see more of those minions get killed in the explosion so I don't have to take them down myself."

Erik nodded. "Yes, let's."

They ventured through the park, careful not to be spotted by the four demons. The minions around them wouldn't know what was up, as they didn't know what they looked like and because they were covered in a salt residue that masked their smell. Luckily Collin had the powers of a demon but not the weaknesses. He could be around Holy water, salt, and he could theoretically be cut by the triduanum knife and not have to worry about it killing him in three days. That hypothesis, however, hadn't been tested.

Kneeling behind a bush, they watched as the four entered the building. They couldn't wait too long in case they realized no humans were inside, but they needed to wait until the minions began piling inside. Once they saw their masters, however, all of them turned to the building, as if programmed, and began filtering in.

Erik nodded toward Elizabeth, who held the trigger.

"Well, here's to victory."

CHAPTER SEVENTEEN

Gwen

Gwen stepped up to the Reichstag building, still captivated by its beauty. It was built in the late 1800s, and the architecture matched just that. Granted, it had been renovated and a dome added after the reunification. It still had that 1800s nostalgia that Gwen admired. Many of the buildings during that area were modeled after the classic Roman and Greek style, making buildings appear grander than they were just so humans could present themselves as better than others in society. It made her grin since to them they were all tools to be used in opening the gates of hell.

Gwen and James stepped inside as Jürgen and Darrell followed, and Gwen tried to sense Collin or the Gargoyles, but she found no trace. The Gargoyles had been using something to mask their stench, but that was no matter. They had the place surrounded. The moment the four of them were in the building, hundreds of minions that were mingling in the area would flock inside the building and around it to make sure they couldn't take any escape routes. They would win this round, no matter the cost.

But first they had to find the members of Parliament and take them down.

Gwen jumped up and down like a giddy schoolgirl. This really was it. They were going to finish them off for good. Berlin was theirs and so would the rest of the world. She glanced up at James, who kissed her.

"Are you ready, my love?"

She nodded. "That I am."

Before they could move forward, Jürgen grabbed her arm. "Wait. Something is wrong."

Gwen glanced around. "I don't see anything. I mean,

all our minions are here, or at least who were outside."

"That's the thing," Jürgen said. "Why are there only minions in here? Where are all the humans?"

Gwen's eyes widened. "Sh—"

Before they could run out the door, the ground shook and loud explosions surrounded them. Gwen felt as if her eardrums had been ruptured from the sound. Everything rang and she couldn't hear anything. Before she knew it, large chucks of glass and marble came crashing down, blocking all the exits. She watched as minion after minion were crushed under the thick pieces. This was their plan—destroy as many of them as they could and have the demons pinned down. James tried to keep close and get them out of the disaster area, but there was no use. They were in the middle of the entry, and too much of the ceiling and upper floors had already crashed down.

A large piece of the ceiling slammed straight into Gwen, and she lost her grip with James. Pain shot through her shoulder and back. She was glad she got her fill of James before coming, otherwise it would have knocked her out cold. With another thud, she felt the chunks crash down on the piece of ceiling that pinned her down.

They had really set them up. She would make the Gargoyles—and Collin—pay.

This reminded her of a few earthquakes through history that she had the unfortunate pleasure of being in the middle of. It was as if God Himself was trying to kill her those times. He probably was or at least was trying to give the Gargoyles an advantage. Fortunately for her, she was always quicker than them. That didn't mean it wasn't close though, and this time she feared that it might be her end.

First, Gwen knew she needed to get out of there and get to some high ground, so to speak. She couldn't let the Gargoyles find her pinned down like this. They would be able to cut off her head or take out her heart for sure. Her heart began to race as she worried about James. They would go after the two of them—it would be the best advantage.

Gwen tried to move her arms but had no luck. The marble was heavy. She used to love marble buildings as they kept out the noises of screams, but now she was missing simple wooden buildings. This wouldn't be the first time she had been caught under rubble, but it was definitely one of the worst situations she had found herself in. She tried moving her legs. They wouldn't budge.

"Damn it," she whispered. She wanted to scream, but she also didn't want the Gargoyles to pinpoint where she was. It was going to take a while to gather enough strength to push these massive chunks off her, and if she was lucky, they wouldn't find her in time.

But they had Collin. He could tell where all of them were.

"Shit, shit, shit." Gwen took a deep breath and tried to calm herself down, but it wasn't working. She needed to do something, otherwise she was a sitting duck.

She couldn't believe they would go to such drastic measures. The entire country was probably in chaos with news crews everywhere outside. If they were going to kill them, they were going to kill them quickly before footage could be taken of them battling.

So Gwen didn't have much time. The question was, should she try to escape, or should she stop resisting and let her energy gain a little before they pulled all this rubble off her. That way, she had some power to fight them with.

The latter was the smarter idea of the two. Gwen took another deep breath and tried to relax enough where her body wasn't getting crushed but not using all her energy to push everything off her. It was only a matter of time before they found her.

She tried to listen for anything, whether it be the Gargoyles or James. She hoped he was all right. She knew in her heart that he was still alive, but she didn't know what state he was in. He could be unconscious, or they could be searching for him first. Gwen prayed that wasn't the case and that he'd somehow made it out of the rubble and was looking for her.

The rubble shifted suddenly, and Gwen prepared herself. She would have to run if it was anyone by another demon. She braced herself as the last rubble moved.

Erik's face was the first thing she saw. Gwen tried to run, but before she knew it, she was held back. She looked back to find Collin holding her. This wasn't good. He was strong, as he'd drunk her blood within twelve hours, and she had lost a lot of blood just now. She pulled and tugged but couldn't free herself.

"Well, Gwen, this is the end," Erik said as he pulled out his sword.

She screamed. "No! Please! Collin, you have to let me go! I can't die!"

"I'm sorry," he whispered. He wasn't letting up. Gwen thrashed around some more, but she was still too weak. This was going to be her end—her creation was going to be her end.

Erik started for her with the sword when suddenly Erik spun and slashed his sword. Gwen realized James had appeared and attacked Erik. Erik swung his sword at James, and he dodged it, but barely. He was slowed down by the lack of energy. She let out a breath she had been holding and tried to pull her arms away from Collin, but he wouldn't budge. She had hoped the distraction would make him loosen his grip, but she was wrong.

"Let me go, Collin!" She growled.

"I can't! You demons need to be destroyed! This is all your fault! Once you're gone, the world will be at peace."

She let out a laugh. "Says who? The Gargoyles? Do you have any idea what Heaven was like for creatures like us? It was torture. We couldn't love who we wanted to love. We had to obey God and do everything he said. It was not the paradise that your churches make it out to be. Well, perhaps for you humans it is. But for us Angels, we are just pawns between light and dark.

And I chose a side that benefited me more."

"You know, in church, the pastor always spoke of how demons spill lies. Now I understand."

"As if the church doesn't lie. Have you seen the horrible things people do in the name of God? It is disgusting. You call demons evil when really humans are the worst creatures of them all. You all have redemption and access to Heaven, but you still do horrible deeds just because they satisfy the present, if even that. Demons don't have a choice—they have to do what they are told."

"So you still have regret?" Collin asked.

Gwen didn't answer but turned her attention back to her love. There was no way James could keep on fighting Erik as blood dripped from his hairline and cuts covered his arms and soaked the now ripped jeans he wore. She had to help him. She had to save him.

Gwen took a deep breath to calm herself down. She would do anything to save the person she loved even if that meant tearing Collin's arms off.

Instead of pulling, she twisted herself around. Collin wasn't prepared for such a maneuver and didn't see what was going to come next. Gwen bit his throat and took in the blood she needed.

CHAPTER EIGHTEEN

Collin

Collin wondered how he could be so stupid. He shoved Gwen back, but she had already taken enough blood to gain a little of her energy back. It wasn't much, but it was enough to heal her wounds.

Crap on a cracker.

She stared at him for a second, then turned her attention to James and Erik. In an instant, she grabbed James and moved back away from them a bit. Collin watched as James bit her neck, taking enough energy to regain his energy but not enough to damage Gwen.

Erik stepped up to him. "Why did you let her go?"

Erik wasn't one to raise his voice, but Collin could sense his frustration. Collin had let him down. He had been distracted, and it was enough for Gwen to get the upper hand and drink some of his blood.

"I'm sorry. It won't happen again."

"Well, it better not since there won't be a next time. Where are the other two demons?"

Collin took a breath. "They are still under the rubble."

"Good. We can try to finish these two before we'll deal with them. Elizabeth should be here soon."

Collin nodded. Elizabeth's task was to take out as many minions as she could outside so they didn't have to worry about them rushing in while they took care of the demons inside. There weren't many that had survived the blast, but she wanted to be safe rather than sorry.

Pulling out his sword, Collin got in a ready stance for whatever the two demons that stood before him had in store for them. They were still weak, but Collin knew not to let his guard down. She tricked him once before.

It wouldn't happen again.

James glared at Collin. "Can we kill him now, my love?"

Gwen's eyes turned yellow. "I think we must."

Although Collin was about to let her die, that comment stung a little. He knew it was coming, however, as he had fully betrayed her. He gulped, knowing that she would never let him drink of her neck again. Even if he survived, the thirst would drive him insane. This was his end, no matter what the outcome was.

Gwen and James split and attacked from both sides. Erik and Collin turned, back-to-back, ready for them. Collin pulled out his water gun full of Holy water. He shot it at James as he came charging at him. It hit him straight in the face, his flesh quickly burning. He hissed and jumped back.

"Are you fucking kidding me?"

This didn't make Gwen falter as she attacked Erik. Erik swung his sword at her, ready to cut off anything he could.

"James, dear, you know what we forgot to bring?"

James was still trying to wipe the Holy water from his face. "What is that?"

"Our swords. Seems these Gargoyles never get with the times. But I wouldn't mind a fun sword fight again."

"Better than this stupid kid and his fucking water gun! He filled it with Holy water!"

Gwen laughed. "It's just water, James. Don't act like such a baby."

"One of you, do me a favor and shoot her with the water gun."

Collin thought about turning and doing just that, but he didn't want his attention to be away from James. This banter was more than likely just a distraction, and Collin couldn't let his guard down.

Erik let out a breath as he put his sword away. "How about instead I just take you up real high? Then James can make fun of your fear of heights."

Gwen tried to back away quickly, but Erik was on her within seconds. He flew up higher and higher. Collin watched as she went higher and higher, and she let out a high-pitched scream.

And two seconds later, Collin realized he shouldn't have looked up. He swung his sword in front of him just as James reached out for his heart. The blade nicked James's arm, but it didn't have enough force to completely cut off his arm. James backed up as he healed the wound.

"Did you really think you could win against me, you stupid human?"

Collin held up his sword and gun. "Maybe not on my own, but with these two weapons, I think I have a good chance."

James narrowed his yellow eyes. "I should have killed you when I had the chance. I let my love for Gwen get the better of me. You see, I let her play with whatever toys she wanted since I know, at the end of the day, it will be her and I together, forever, our blood forever combined."

Collin frowned. "You think I still want Gwen? Maybe she's right. You're just a jealous boyfriend."

James hissed. "And I have every right to be. You think you can just waltz in, after thousands of years of us being together, and think that she would pick you? *You?* You are a weakling—a human who can't comprehend what true love is. You are just an ant, and we are giants that control the world."

Collin noted he was getting a lot angrier than he should be. Perhaps he was jealous. "Seems to me you're just snakes eating the dust of the earth, forever chained down and will never get the chance to see Heaven again."

James rushed straight for him. Collin pulled the trigger on his gun. It hit James and burned his skin. James hissed and jumped back.

"Face me like a man!"

"No! You will kill me!"

"That's the point!"

Collin pointed up with his sword. "Shouldn't you be figuring a way to get Gwen back down from there? Aren't you worried?"

James glanced up, and Collin took the chance to charge him and swung his sword. James was able to get out of the way from the fatal blow to his neck but not fast enough where he didn't come out unscathed. James had a giant slash in his chest. James touched the wound as blood came dripping out of it. He licked his fingers.

"I wonder, since Gwen's blood is coursing through my veins, if you can become so bloodthirsty when you smell my blood."

Collin's eyes widened. The place had been filled with the aroma of blood that Collin hadn't noticed. James was right. There was a small part of Gwen's scent coming off him. It called to him, and he wanted to devour it.

He tightened his grip on his sword and began hacking away at him. "Shut up!"

James laughed as he moved back faster than Collin could move forward. "Humans will always be weak, even hybrid ones. And minions are just pathetic, but they add to our numbers. Speaking of which, you must have killed most of the ones we created, huh? I swore we had more."

"That we did," Collin said as he kept hacking. "But you still didn't notice anything was up."

"Oh, we knew something was up. But we never imagined the Gargoyles would go to such extremes. Seems we underestimated them. They are capable of as much destruction as we are."

"They didn't let anyone die in the explosion. They used their powers to make everyone stay away."

"Ah, well that explains a lot. But don't go on thinking they are so innocent. They did make Gwen create you, after all. They knew for years and kept it from you. You should have died that night when I killed you."

Collin stopped slashing, and James stopped. He had a point. They didn't seem to have any problem turning him. James slowly stepped forward.

"You know, I'm sure our Dark Lord could grant any wish you want if you helped us defeat the Gargoyles here and now. You could have a harem of humans, or demons, or whatever you want. Money, power, women. You name it, he would grant it."

Collin wanted none of those things. All he wanted was to go back to his pub to a time where he didn't know about the battle between demons and Angels— back to when he thought humans were all that was left in the world and demons were just used to scare children into being good.

He wanted to go back to a simpler time when he was in love with a cute girl with beautiful red hair.

James reached out in a flash and grabbed the sword by the blade. His hands bled as he pulled it to him, laughing. "So easy. Humans can be so fickle. Make them think of something they want and they are easily distracted."

Collin squirted the Holy water straight into James's face. He screeched as Collin made a run for it. James now had a weapon, and this wasn't going to be good. Before he could attack him with the sword, a loud thud resonated through the area. Both Collin's and James's attention turned to find that the noise had been Gwen. Erik had thrown her down from the clouds, or she had done something to make him drop her.

She coughed up blood and tried to move but was still weak from having a building crash down on her. James was about to run to her when another figure appeared above Gwen. It was Elizabeth.

Elizabeth pointed her sword at Gwen's heart. "I am happy to find that I'll be your end."

With that, Elizabeth slashed her sword down at Gwen.

CHAPTER NINETEEN

James

James screamed. *No, this couldn't be happening*, he thought. He couldn't lose her. She was everything to James—this couldn't be her end. If she died, there was no point in living.

Just as Elizabeth thrust her sword, a figure appeared and grabbed her arm. It was Darrell. Thank the Dark Lord he got out from under the rubble just in time. James hurried toward Gwen and Darrell when he felt acid hit his skin. He hissed and turned to find Collin standing next to him.

"You aren't getting any closer."

He was about to attack the boy with his sword when Erik dropped down next to Collin.

James grinned. "Well, looks like we'll have another sword fight. It has been a while. When was the last time? In the presence of Queen Victoria herself."

"I believe so." Erik raised his sword. "En garde."

In a situation like this, all was fair in a sword fight. James didn't care about form or rules, like those that are made in sports. All that mattered was destroying an opponent, which is exactly what James was going to do. He swung hard and fast at Erik, careful to make sure to block Erik's swings and to counter them with his own swings, a kick, or push his body toward him, all the while keeping an eye on Gwen.

Together with Darrell, they seemed to be able to hold Elizabeth off even if she had a sword. Darrell was weak, however, as he'd just gotten out from under the rubble, and Gwen had fallen from the clouds themselves.

Something stung James's back, and he growled. Collin was still there with his stupid water gun. Collin squirted again, and James was ready to slice him through with the sword when Erik took a swing at him. James blocked it just in time, but not before Collin squirted him again.

"Stop that!" James yelled.

"Why? Does it sting?" Collin grinned.

James kicked Erik back and turned his attention on the hybrid. Collin jumped back as James ran at him with the sword. Collin stumbled upon the rubble and fell down to his knees.

"Say goodbye, you pest!"

James began to swing his sword at the hybrid's neck when he felt a sword pierce through his stomach. Blood came gushing up and out of his mouth. He looked down to find the sharp end of a sword jutting out of his torso. Glancing back, he found Erik had thrown the sword from where he was. James reached back and pulled out the sword with a laugh.

"Great. Now I have two swords."

Erik charged at him, faster than James could react. He dropped both the swords as Erik pulled him up in the sky. He thrashed around, but it was no use. He felt the chains around his ankle burn hotter and hotter, and it was as if he were going to be ripped apart. James hissed and growled, but Erik didn't seem to care. They were going to use any means necessary to weaken the demons. James did not like the current odds.

They hit the cloud layer, and James felt as if his leg was on fire. Although this was the same height that airplanes flew, James was weak and hadn't fed right beforehand. The pain was worse—almost unbearable.

Then Erik threw him down, and James felt as if he were a missile, heading straight for where the others awaited. He hit the rubble, causing an explosion of dust. Something sliced into his back.

He lost consciousness for a moment as everything spun around him and appeared to darken. He kept blinking, trying to regain his senses. He turned his head to find Gwen getting up with Darrell's help, coughing and trying to get away from Elizabeth, who had been knocked over by James's collision. At least he stopped whatever she was going to do.

Now that he had more of his bearings, James tried to stand but found something tugging at his body. He peered down to find pieces of rebar jutting out of his torso. They had barely missed his heart.

Getting out of this was going to hurt a lot more than he was able to bear. He was weak and needed blood. He used more strength to try to get up, but he didn't have any energy left. He was a sitting duck, and he knew it.

Collin stepped up to James, a sword in his hand—more than likely the one that James had dropped.

James shook his head. "Of all the people, why did it have to be you to give me the final blow?"

Collin stared down at him. "It seems fitting, don't you think? You killed me once, and now I'll kill you."

James kept trying to move, but there was no use—he was pinned down. Collin lifted his sword, but just as he did, something tackled him to the ground. James blinked a few times, still trying to adjust his eyes to everything. It took all that he had not to lose consciousness again.

It had been Jürgen. He finally got out from under the rubble, but he was injured as bad as Darrell. James turned his attention back to Gwen to find Elizabeth stalking her and Darrell. Both of them were too weak to put up a fight. All of them were too weak.

Was this going to be the end? Were the Gargoyles really going to win this war? Seth was still alive, so they had that. But would Seth be able to take down two Gargoyles and a hybrid all by himself? More than likely not. The four of them were supposed to do some damage, but the Gargoyles had dealt the damage.

Jürgen was having a hard time fending off Collin. Luckily Jürgen had picked up the other sword that he'd lost, but he wasn't much of a match for Collin, who still had most of his health other than the energy Gwen had drained from him.

A shadow appeared above James. He peered up to find an Angel coming down from the sky. It was Erik. Yup, this was going to be his end. He had no one to rescue him, and he had no way of moving.

They should have thought this plan out more, but they never would have expected the Gargoyles to go to such drastic measures. They had blown up Parliament, and now the entire European Union was probably in chaos. James supposed it was better than losing the war and having the entire world taken over by demons, at least in the Gargoyles' view. James turned his head back to Gwen. She struggled to get moving over the rubble, to get to him and away from Elizabeth. She reached her hand out to him, and James lifted his hand a little, as if he could reach her. He couldn't.

Elizabeth was behind her and began to swing at Gwen's throat. Tears filled James's eyes. Was he going to witness his love killed right in front of him? At least his own life would soon be taken, and they could suffer hell together.

"Gwen!" He screamed just as Elizabeth was about to cut off her head when the unthinkable happened. Darrell jumped in front of the sword and shoved Gwen out of the way. James watched as Darrell's head rolled off his body and his entire body turned into dust.

Gwen screamed. "No! Darrell!"

James couldn't believe it. Darrell had sacrificed himself for Gwen. Although they were best friends, it was rare for a demon to sacrifice themselves for anyone. Was it because they were friends, or had it been because Darrell knew if he or Gwen died, that the other would be too weak?

Did it even matter? James didn't expect any of them to make it out alive. Erik was now upon him, and he didn't think he would have much luck getting out of this one. Elizabeth was still in front of Gwen as Gwen cried and screamed at Elizabeth.

James turned his attention back to Jürgen; he was barely keeping his own against Collin. Collin had that stupid water gun, and Jürgen appeared to be drenched in Holy water. James tried to move again, but he couldn't get his body out of the rebar. His energy was draining fast.

Their end was interrupted with a loud noise. James peered up to find two helicopters circling above them. Suddenly bullets came raining down upon them. None hit the demons, but it was enough for the Gargoyles to jump back. James took a deep breath. They were minions. The helicopters were sent by Seth. He must have contacted the local military that they had under their power the moment he saw the Parliament blow up.

The minions who were shooting their guns were careful to aim at the Gargoyles and Collin and not hit James or the other demons. Jürgen, who no longer had to fend off Collin, turned his attention back on James. He limped over with Gwen and helped pull James out of the rebar. James let out a scream as one of the metal pieces scraped his heart.

One of the helicopters landed near them, and they hurried to board. All three of them collapsed inside as the helicopter rose back up, raining bullets all around to fend off the Gargoyles. James tried to stay conscious and watch as they retreated to wherever Seth wanted them next, but he had no energy left.

Everything went black.

CHAPTER TWENTY

Erik

Bullets sprayed the area, and Erik jumped back before he could get shot. Granted, he wouldn't die, but it would still hurt, and he didn't want to be weakened when he didn't know what was going to happen next. The demons weren't ones to retreat; it was usually the Gargoyles that had to retreat even if they took down a demon or two.

Never before now did Erik want to curse so bad.

They had all four demons within their grasps, but they had failed. They destroyed one demon, however, that sacrificed his life for Gwen's. Erik never knew a demon to sacrifice himself without something in return. Perhaps the demon knew that this was the end, or perhaps he really did care about Gwen. Erik had seen that demon before with Gwen and James, many times throughout history actually. Perhaps they were dear friends.

Erik watched as the three demons that were left boarded the helicopter. That would be one painful ride, as they would be away from the ground, weakened, with their shackles burning. It served them right.

More bullets hit the ground around them, and Erik jumped back, using his wings to leap quicker and higher. Collin took cover, using his quick speed behind some of the rubble. Collin couldn't fly like he and Elizabeth could, so he was going to be stuck there for quite some time. Erik caught sight of Elizabeth and hopped over to her. He had a plan, but he needed her help for it.

Elizabeth seemed to know what he wanted to say as he pointed up at the helicopter. The machines were loud —something that Erik always hated. Why did humans always make machines so loud?

He nodded to Elizabeth. They would use their powers over flight to try to take the two helicopters down. It wouldn't be easy, and Erik wasn't sure it would be possible, but they had to try. The demons were weak, and they couldn't just let them retreat without putting up a fight.

Erik and Elizabeth focused on taking down the closest helicopter that was providing cover for the helicopter that held the demons. They wouldn't get anywhere with the demons shooting at them the entire time.

Bullets came raining down upon them quicker than Erik had wished for. He dodged them by flying in a sporadic route toward the helicopter. Erik never could remember all the technical terms for different types of helicopters and planes. He considered them all uncivilized, along with guns and other weapons. Swords he kept since it was easier to slice off a demon's head with them. Then again, he despised bombs as well, but they had used them for the surprise attack.

Normally the Gargoyles tried not to attract attention by flying in the air, especially since the inventions of cameras were rather instant. They didn't need the entire world panicking. They flew more in the olden days when not many would see them, and it would only be rumors that spread and not all the people would exactly believe him. But with video footage, it was a little harder. And everyone had a phone on them that could capture a moment. Modern humans thought they were freer when, in reality, they were trapped with constantly being monitored by each other. It was quite sad to watch.

Erik and Elizabeth got closer to the helicopter. They tried to outrun them, but Elizabeth and Erik were faster. Even with the bullets pouring down at them, they were able to catch up. Before the minions could react, they ripped open the side door and jumped inside. A dozen demons awaited them, hissing and baring their fangs, but they had no chance against the Gargoyles. Erik grabbed one after another, ripping them apart and throwing them out of the helicopter. Elizabeth swung her sword and destroyed every minion that was near her and took out the pilots.

Elizabeth grabbed the controls and made the helicopter go higher in the sky. Erik located a missile that the minions didn't use and grabbed an automatic rifle. As they jumped out, making distance from the helicopter, they shot up the missile and the helicopter exploded. Now they didn't have to worry about a large machine falling down on the city. Granted, pieces from the helicopter would fall, but they would do less damage than the entire thing intact.

Erik threw away the automatic rifle. He didn't want to be associated with such uncivilized weapons. Turning to their next objective, they headed toward the demons.

The second helicopter, which held the demons, was quite far off by the time they were able to shift their attention away. They weren't holding back with their weapons either. They shot at Erik and Elizabeth, never letting up and not trying to guess where they might fly. They covered the entire sky with bullets and watched as the city was sprayed with violence. Erik's heart felt as if it were going to drop out of his chest. Countless lives were being lost because of this fight, but he couldn't let up. If they succeeded in getting to the demons, they might be able to take them out once and for all.

Erik and Elizabeth moved on toward the helicopter. A few bullets grazed his arms, but he didn't falter. As long as they weren't wings, they were okay.

The two of them were gaining on the helicopter. Erik could taste victory when the last thing he expected dropped out of the helicopter. It was two missiles.

He and Elizabeth stopped flying toward the helicopter. Erik turned to her. "We can't let that drop on the city! It will kill thousands upon thousands of people!"

"But we have come so far. Are we really going to lose our chance in destroying them for these humans?"

Erik didn't know the answer to that, but he didn't know if he could live with himself with so many deaths. He had seen countless wars erupt due to their wars—he had seen how many humans lost their lives because of the demons. He didn't want to see any more added.

Erik went after one of the missiles, and Elizabeth sighed and went after the other. Erik was able to pull it back up from hitting the city and flew it up into the air. He would have to find someplace that didn't have any humans to destroy it.

Or, Erik found out, this had been a diversion. Suddenly bullets rained down upon him and the missile. He couldn't believe he had been so stupid.

The bullets hit the missile, and the explosion threw him back and into the city below. His body burned and he was in agonizing pain, but at least he was still alive. He just prayed they wouldn't circle back around to finish the job.

Elizabeth, who had caught on quicker than Erik had, let her missile fly in the air as she let go and went after him. Hers exploded from the bullets, but she was far enough away by the time it went up in a fiery explosion.

Elizabeth flew down and caught him right before he hit the ground. Now he knew that they wouldn't circle back for him—Elizabeth still had all her strength.

"That was a close one, Erik. You should have just let them go."

Erik shook his head, which was a mistake as he was pretty sure he messed up his spine. "I had to help the city. I wouldn't be able to live with myself if I had known I caused so many deaths."

"No, the demons cause all the deaths in this war. None of this is our fault."

He knew she had a point, but he couldn't help but feel guilty. Because of them, all of Berlin, if not the entire European Union, was in chaos seeing all this destruction televised. There were probably videos of them flying through the air, just like there had been in

London. Many people thought it to be a hoax, and many others believed it was a sign of the end times. They weren't wrong.

"What are we going to do next?"

"Well, to be honest, I'm not sure. They won't be falling for something like this again. They are probably going to ready themselves as best as possible with loads of human weapons. If they are all regrouping, however, at least they will be in one spot. There are four left, and two of us… Whatever we think of, it's going to have to be good."

Erik knew she was going to say that. He could tell that she felt this was going to be their only chance and that they had lost it. He tried not to think about it, however, as it only discouraged him. Discouragement only led to more failure. One had to keep their head up high if they wanted to succeed.

Elizabeth landed down where Collin awaited them on the rubble that was once the Parliament building. He furrowed his brows.

"I take it since I am still alive that Gwen is too."

Erik nodded. Another regret. "They escaped, but we got one demon. The odds are lowering."

Elizabeth folded her arms. "We should have gotten

all of them. They were within our grasps, and if it weren't for those helicopters, we would have won. If there wasn't another demon out there calling the shots, we would have won."

Erik let out a breath. "There is no benefit from thinking about what things could have been. We need to focus on what to do next, and better yet"—he grimaced —"I need to heal up. I should be fine in a day, but I don't want to be caught by them in this state."

Elizabeth nodded. "Right, you don't want to be caught in the same state that we had them."

Erik chuckled, which hurt the most. But she was right. They were at their weakest point, and the two of them still lost. Was there going to be a way to defeat them now that they were on their guard? They also had to deal with the fact that Collin wouldn't be able to get any of Gwen's blood, as she would probably kill him on the spot. Would Collin survive? Would he be able to stomach their blood now or be able to drink from a human?

Everything was up in the air now, but that was how it always was for them.

CHAPTER TWENTY-ONE

Gwen

Gwen watched as the Gargoyles retreated. It appeared that Erik was badly wounded from that explosion. He was probably weak, and there was a chance the demons could take him down.

She stood up and winced. That was a lie—she hurt like hell. There wasn't a part of her that didn't burn with pain. Her skin was torn; her blood soaked her clothes and Converse. How could she have been so stupid? Why didn't she realize what kind of trap they had set up for them?

"What do you think you're doing?" Jürgen growled.

Gwen shot him a look. "Erik is weak—I can take him out."

"No, you cannot. Elizabeth is still with him. She would kill you in an instant, and James would be weak enough for them to take down too. That would be three of us dead."

Gwen's eyes filled with tears. Darrell was dead. He had sacrificed himself to save her. She couldn't believe it. Did he do it because she knew the Gargoyles would take down James as well, or did he not want to see his friend dead? Gwen didn't care the answer. She just wanted to avenge his death.

"You need to help James. Do you have any blood you can spare?"

Gwen peered down at James. He was still bleeding from the wounds he sustained when he was pierced by the rebar. She didn't have much energy left, but she could give enough to stop his bleeding.

She bit her wrist and knelt down to James's body. She put her wrist to his lips and let the dark red liquid drip into his mouth. Moments later he began to stir.

Gwen moved her wrist before his instincts kicked in and he attacked her. Normally she wouldn't care, but she was quite weak herself.

James's eyes flickered open—glowing yellow. He appeared as if he were about to attack. Gwen placed her hand on his chest.

"James, calm down. We are in the clear."

He was breathing heavily, and a few moments had passed until he finally had a normal movement to his chest. He blinked a few times, but the yellow didn't go away. He was still too hungry.

"What happened?" he croaked. "Did Darrell really…?"

Gwen nodded. "They killed him." Tears started streaming down her eyes as she collapsed on his chest. The teardrops mixed with the blood that soaked his clothes.

James grunted but didn't move her. He patted her back. "It's all right; we can bring him back. We just have to open the door."

"What if we fail? What if we don't succeed?" Gwen asked.

"We'll win. We have to."

"I'm going to kill her. I'm going to kill that bitch."

James rubbed her back. "In due time, my sweetheart, in due time."

Jürgen coughed. "Sorry to interrupt whatever this crap is, but we need to make a pit stop. I don't know about you both, but I am famished."

She nodded. "I need food. Bad. I haven't been this hungry since… Well, since you shot me in the back, Jürgen."

Jürgen grunted. "You deserved it. Besides, a couple of bullets wouldn't have harmed you that much if it weren't for the fact you hadn't had human blood for so long."

"Touché. Well then, should we land somewhere and get a bite to eat?"

Jürgen went up to the pilots and requested just that. It would be a few hours before they would arrive in Moscow with the helicopter. Gwen didn't think she could last that long without devouring something—probably the minions that had saved them. Although she didn't really care for minions one way or another, she would feel a little bit bad to destroy the creatures that had saved her. It wouldn't keep her up at night though.

Gwen kissed James on the lips. He raised an

eyebrow. "What was that for?"

"I thought I was going to lose you."

He lifted his hand and stroked her cheek. "I thought I was going to lose you. But we are alive and we are fine."

"For now."

James shook his head. "They will not be able to get the jump on us like that again. They lost their chance. They won't win this war."

"And we will. Then everything will be back to normal. Darrell will be back on Earth, Lucifer will rule the land, and we'll see our friends again." Gwen said those words, but she wasn't sure how much she believed them. Something in her gut still worried. What if there was no hope for them? What if what was promised was a lie and that Lucifer just destroyed them in the end?

Jürgen reappeared. "The minions are going to land us near a small village outside of Łódź. Only a few hundred people in population. We can drink to our heart's content."

Gwen and James grinned, ready to have their fill. It had been quite some time since she had massacred an entire village. She missed having such fun.

About thirty minutes later they landed. She helped James limp off the helicopter as curious men slowly came up to the helicopter. *Curiosity killed the cat*, Gwen always said.

A couple of men started asking in Polish who they were and what was going on.

Jürgen answered. "It's nothing to worry about. We just need some supplies. But if you could be so kind and help our friend here. He is struggling to walk."

Two of the men walked over to help James when James launched at their throats. The humans screamed as he bit into them. They didn't need minions, so they were completely devouring the blood of all the humans that they could find.

Gwen attacked the other human that offered to help James before he could try to run, adrenaline filling her body. Her feral instincts to hunt to survive kicked in— just like when they first were dropped onto Earth all those centuries ago. She was acting completely on animal instincts—an animal who was hungry and needed to feed.

She remembered those days like they were yesterday —when humans weren't civilized, or at least organized. She didn't think humans were at all civilized but lied to themselves so they could feel superior when really they just had different ideals in different cultures. Thousands of years had passed, and they always acted the same. Gwen didn't know if that was a good thing or a bad thing. At least they were predictable.

Gwen let the bloodlust devour her soul or whatever she had that was the equivalent of a soul. All she could see was red—the color of passion. She wanted more than anything to keep devouring and devouring until every square inch of this town was covered in the crimson color.

She wanted the Gargoyles to find her painting and realize it was their fault—they had provoked her and now these humans would pay the price.

Gwen imagined all the humans to appear like Elizabeth. All she could see was that rotten Gargoyle in front of her as she bit and drank the blood of each and every human around her. Their screams were music to Gwen's ears as she envisioned what Elizabeth would sound like screaming as she slowly ripped off each finger and each toe and each limb. Then ever so slowly she would reach into her chest and pull her heart out.

Grinning at the image in her mind, Gwen ripped out more and more throats as she laughed. She glanced over at James, who was also releasing his anger about what the Gargoyles had done to them. Even Jürgen appeared to be having fun, but then again, he was once called Vlad the Impaler. Most of the areas throughout Eastern Europe shudder at his name. He never let up, even for people who pled for their lives.

One after one they killed the humans in the village. They didn't know if they'd gotten all of them, nor did they care. News would get out from anyone stopping by about how nearly an entire village had been destroyed, and she would let Erik deal with the remorse. It served him right.

They tried to go after their helicopter. Only due to not wanting to cause any more destruction in Berlin did they let up. Gwen saw it with her own eyes—the missile had blown up in his face. She wished she could have gotten a closer picture. Hell, she wished she could have finished the job. It was no matter, however. She would see his demise. Hopefully she was the one to deal it.

Gwen headed back to the helicopter and found James and Jürgen already waiting for her. James stepped up to her.

"You missed a spot." He licked her check and kissed

her. It felt good to have so much energy back. Although she didn't appreciate how close she was to death, dealing with that much was a little euphoric, especially once energy was restored and the entire village was wiped off the map.

They got into the helicopter, and Gwen watched as the village, now painted red, became smaller and smaller in the distance. How many more would be dyed in such a color once Lucifer was released? She wondered if he wanted to destroy it all or become ruler. Perhaps it was both.

James leaned over and kissed her cheek. "Don't worry, my love. We'll get our revenge. We'll open the gates of hell, and we'll be rolling in riches."

She grinned. "Yes. I cannot wait."

CHAPTER TWENTY-TWO

Collin

Collin helped Elizabeth assist Erik back to the hotel room. They were able to escape past the officers and news crews, but not without Elizabeth using her powers of persuasion. Although Collin had seen them use it dozens of times now, it was still fascinating to watch. All she had to do was tell someone to do something, and they would do it—like a Jedi in *Star Wars*. He was very, very glad the demons couldn't do such things, especially since in most movies, the bad guy could use such powers. Collin had a feeling if they could, this war would have already been over.

People frantically ran through the streets, and cars were stopped in traffic as everyone tried to either find their loved ones or tried to leave the city until everything was figured out. Collin wondered if the hotel they were heading back to would still be open. It would probably be unlocked at the very least, and they could go to their room.

Not only were people frantically running away, others used this time to break into businesses and begin looting. Collin wished he could help those businesses, but he had a feeling things wouldn't go back to normal for quite some time. Shards of the helicopter and missile had done a lot of damage to the buildings around the area. Collin couldn't believe a city could become so chaotic so quickly. But this city had seen a lot over the centuries. It would move forward—that is, as long as the Gargoyles won. Otherwise, none of this mattered.

To Collin's surprise, the hotel was still operating, but many people were leaving keys at the desk and getting the heck out of town. He was glad that most of the employees were busy and didn't see the state Erik was in. To normal humans, he would need an ambulance and to be taken to a hospital ASAP. His skin had third- and fourth-degree burns scattered throughout his body, and chunks of metal were still sticking out of his skin. He had healed quite a bit since they started walking, but it was still a grotesque sight to see.

Collin himself wasn't great to look at either. Blood crusted the base of his neck where Gwen had bitten him, and he had a few scratch marks and bullet wounds from the minions. Most were healed up, but the blood was still there as it had soaked his clothes and clung to his skin. He hated the feeling of blood-encrusted clothing.

They arrived to the hotel room, and Erik collapsed on the couch. He moaned a little, as he was now putting pressure on the wounds.

Collin wasn't sure what he could do to help. For burns like those, ice was actually worse. Then again, if those wounds were on a human, he wouldn't even be alive.

"What do you want me to do?" Collin asked. "I feel sort of helpless."

Erik shook his head. "There isn't anything you can

do right now. I'll heal eventually and will be fine. You should rest up and heal as well. We have a long road ahead of us."

Collin nodded. "Right. I can do that."

He left them in the living area. Elizabeth wasn't going to rest but was pacing back and forth. Collin didn't like seeing her as frustrated as he knew it was because she felt that this was a failure of a mission. He let out a sigh as he closed the door.

Peeling off his clothes, Collin wondered how it was possible to be so close to victory and yet fail so miserably. He wondered if he had been more careful with Gwen—if he hadn't let her bite his neck—if they would have won. Was he the reason the mission failed?

Collin collapsed on the bed. He knew it probably wasn't his fault entirely, but he couldn't help but feel responsible. If he was stronger—if he hadn't let his emotions get in his way—he wouldn't have messed up.

He let out a moan in his pillow. He should have killed Gwen when he had the chance. He had a sword. He could have easily cut off her head. But he didn't. He couldn't.

When it came down to it, he didn't know if he could kill Gwen. He could hold her back while one of the

Gargoyles did it, but he couldn't kill her. There was no way.

Was it because he still had feelings for her? Or was it one of those cases where a creation couldn't destroy his master? He had a feeling it was probably his own heart stopping him. Even though she had shattered his heart —shattered his life—he didn't know if he could bring her end.

He shook his head. This wasn't what he should be thinking about right now. He should be resting and focusing on what to do next, not thinking about her. But watching her as Elizabeth destroyed her friend, he had never seen her in such pain and anger. And she more than likely blamed him for that demon's death.

Collin was hungry, and he wondered if he was ever going to be able to feed again. Gargoyle blood didn't satisfy his needs, and he had a feeling human blood wouldn't either. Collin wondered if he would ever reach a point where he would be willing to test that theory. Minions did nothing to fill him. The only person who could help him was Gwen, but he knew he wouldn't be able to go to her anytime soon.

James had mentioned that his blood could satisfy him, but Collin knew that wasn't an option on the table.

He had pissed the demon off during the fight, not to mention he already hated him for stealing his girl. Collin didn't believe he actually had ever stolen her, rather he was just something to quench her boredom when she was on her own. Perhaps he was wrong, but it didn't matter now. Now she was trying to bring the destruction of the world and open the gates of hell.

Taking a few deep breaths, Collin tried to push everything that had happened behind him. Worrying about such things would get him nowhere. He needed to focus on the future and to let his wounds heal on their own without the helped of Gwen's blood.

He heard mumbles come from the other side of his door. He listened, trying to make out the words that Erik and Elizabeth said.

"Erik, you know that was our only chance, right?" Elizabeth asked. "There is no way that we'll get the upper hand again. We have failed. We have let our brothers and sisters down."

"Don't say that. We aren't dead. There is no reason to give up hope."

"We pissed off Gwen. You remember how she gets when you piss her off? She gets violent. I don't even want to check the news to see what town they destroyed. Knowing them, they are going to stop somewhere and slaughter a whole village. They have done it before after a battle like this."

Collin felt sick to his stomach. It was one thing to see them slaughter an entire bar, but an entire village just for the fun of it? Not to make minions, just to kill. Granted, they probably needed to feed after their battle, but a whole town seemed excessive.

"We'll follow them and we'll take them all down. We have to, Elizabeth. Otherwise, why were we given an impossible task? Why was the fate of the world in our hands?"

"Because our Lord has more faith in us than we deserve? Because he actually thought we would succeed? Instead, we are going to go back to Heaven as failures. Do you know what it will be like for us? Everyone is going to know us twelve as the twelve who disappointed God. Are you really ready for that?"

There was a pause before Erik answered, "He won't be disappointed in us. We have done all that we could. If he really wanted us to win, he would have sent down more than twelve."

"Exactly! It doesn't make sense, Erik! He has the power to just wipe the demons out of existence! What is all this stupid war stuff even for? We have suffered in his name, and I am beginning to wonder what the entire point has been. Are the humans that special that he wants them to stand up in this war and fight? This entire time, should we have told all the humans who we were and what we needed to do?"

Collin could tell this was a conversation they had before. He couldn't imagine the frustration of battling like this over and over again for two thousand years. He had to admit, he didn't quite understand the point either. He thought it was because he was a human, but perhaps it was because it was more complicated even for them to understand.

"You know that the demons would have just slaughtered all the humans if that was the case. This is a war between good and evil, Elizabeth. You know that. The sides have to play fair. Our Lord has to show that goodness has nothing to do with power but do what is right for the sake of light."

"The demons never play fair though. They gain power from corruption. It makes you wonder sometimes…"

"What do you mean?" Erik asked.

"Never mind. It doesn't matter anymore. We'll rest

up and follow them to Russia. I presume they are going back to where the other demon is to regroup, then they will all be together and we can take them down once and for all."

They stopped talking, and Collin sighed. This was not looking good for them, but at least they all would be in the same spot. For all Collin knew, perhaps they would be able to trap all the demons again, and they would win this war soon.

Deep in his heart though, he knew that wasn't going to happen. The next part of the war would just bring more frustration and bloodshed.

CHAPTER TWENTY-THREE

James

James wrapped his arm around Gwen as they rode in the helicopter toward Moscow. He felt great after devouring that entire village. It hit just the spot. He noticed that Gwen had a good time as well and was able to let off some steam, but now that she was confined to this helicopter, her body was tensing up.

"We should be there within a couple of hours, my love. Then you can pace around."

She let off a brief laugh. "You know as well as I that no amount of pacing will help me deal with this anger."

"Well then…" He kissed the side of her head, her red hair soft against his blood. "We'll just make those two Gargoyles pay."

"Oh, we will. We shall go after Elizabeth first. She was the one who killed Darrell, and I have a feeling she was the one who orchestrated the entire operation. Unfortunately for her, it didn't work, and now she will pay the price."

"Don't get ahead of yourself," Jürgen grunted.

James was surprised he could hear them from the other side of the helicopter with how loud it was. He also was acting as if he was sleeping as his eyes were closed and he was leaning back in his chair. "We'll have to see what Seth wants to do first. He might want to go after Erik or leave Russia entirely before another battle."

Gwen pursed her lips. She didn't like that idea, James knew. Gwen was a person who when she wanted revenge, would act upon that need. She hadn't ever been unsuccessful either, which was good since waiting was not her strong suit.

"But she will die soon enough, Gwen, you can count

on that."

"I want to rip her head off. No, I want to torture her until she can't stand it any longer and then watch as she cries out to her God. I want her to resent ever being sent down to Earth. I want her to forsake everything that is Holy and then crush her heart with my own hands."

James smiled. "You know, it really turns me on when you talk like that. I love you and your sadistic mind."

He kissed her, and she wrapped her arms around him.

"Knock it off. I'm still on this helicopter too, you know." Jürgen opened one of his eyes and glared at them.

Gwen backed off and stuck her tongue at him. "Just keep your eyes closed then. And stop listening in."

"I can't. You two are too loud."

She rolled her eyes and folded her arms like some teenager being called out by an adult. That made James chuckle.

"Don't worry, my love. We'll find ourselves a nice hotel in Moscow."

"We better. Or else we might annoy king of the world over there."

Jürgen shot her one more look and went back to closing his eyes. Gwen leaned her head on him.

"I'm so furious, James. He was my best friend."

"I know. We'll revive him though. Don't worry."

"It should have been me, shouldn't it have been? I was the one who caused all this. We should have already won."

James didn't know how to respond. She was right. It was her fault that they hadn't already destroyed the Gargoyles. They had a trap set up, and she sprang it early, causing the Gargoyles to flee. They were able to take a couple down, but many fled, not to mention they'd lost demons. If she had kept her doubts to herself, they would be in paradise—or at least what was paradise for them.

So James didn't say anything and held her tighter. He also didn't speak because he knew he would say something to piss her off, such as "Well yeah, if you didn't betray us," or "That's what happens when you fall for a human." Keeping quiet was the best method of action, especially since he wanted a bit of her blood that night.

He was surprised, however, that Jürgen didn't interject. Normally he would, but perhaps he was as tired as they were. Although the blood filled them up, that didn't mean they weren't tired of everything that had happened. That surprise attack was not something they had seen coming.

They needed to rest and meet with Seth. Hopefully the Gargoyles would also rest. James was surprised they didn't fly after them. Then again, they might have, but he had passed out. Then he remembered there were two helicopters, not just theirs. Perhaps they did try but failed. If they were able to take out a Gargoyle though, Jürgen or Gwen would have told them. Either way, James figured they would need some time to heal and figure out what to do next.

James closed his eyes and let his mind drift off as they kept forward toward Moscow.

Hours passed and when James opened his eyes again, he found that they had arrived in Moscow. Gwen was staring down at the city, waiting patiently as she probably had plans she wanted to bring up to Seth. He stretched, and she turned to him.

"Good morning, sleepyhead. Did you get some rest?"

He laughed. It was well into the evening hours in Russia, but to them it was like a new day. "I think I did just that. What about you? Did you get any rest?"

She turned her attention back down to the city. "A

little. I don't think I'll feel any better until I see that bitch pay."

She was in one of her obsessive moods. At least this time it was in their favor. James prayed that she wouldn't turn her allegiance again, although he really doubted that would happen—not after what they had done to her.

They landed on the top of a skyscraper and found Seth waiting for them. His bleached hair was gelled back, and he wore a long leather coat. His blue eyes scanned them. He frowned when he finished counting.

"Don't tell me…"

Gwen's eyes gazed down, not wanting to see the fury in his face. He stepped forward and slapped her. James reached out, but Jürgen grabbed his wrist to stop him.

"This is your fault, Gwen! You know that, don't you? If it weren't for you, all this would be over! His death and our failures are on your head! And I am sure when the next time Lucifer sees you, he will make sure you understand that."

She nodded slowly but still didn't look up. Seth grabbed her by the chin and forced her to make eye contact.

"You understand that, right?" he repeated.

Gwen nodded. "Yes, sir. I do."

"Good. Then you will be careful to follow my orders."

Seth let go of her jaw and turned toward the door, his trench coat making him look even more dramatic. Although Gwen was known to cause a lot of problems and mischief, Seth was known for making everything more dramatic than it needed to be.

They followed him inside. Gwen stayed quiet, not wanting to get on his bad side again. She and Seth hadn't been face-to-face since she came back to them. He had a feeling there was going to be a lot of smack talk, just as there usually was when they video called him. James sighed, not wanting to deal with so much drama. Perhaps if he was too dramatic, James would start playing "Drama Queen" by Lindsay Lohan to make him shut up or be even angrier with him. Either way, it would be fun to see his reaction.

They used the elevator to travel down a few floors and arrived at a business floor. It seemed that Seth had already gotten things under control in Russia, or at least that was what James figured with the scent of minions. Russia had always been an easy grab for them. Sometimes they didn't even have to use minions to take over the government. They either just asked the leaders or were able to start a revolution.

They entered a meeting room and took a seat at the table. It was a standard-looking business room, surrounded by windows with a large table that was either made of wood or some weird stuff that James didn't quite understand. The chairs could be comfy or not, depending the country. These were quite comfy. Seth made sure of that. Most countries carried out business the same or at least in the first-world countries. He preferred the olden days when they would sit in a circle around a fire and discuss plans with the fire lighting up their faces like shadows. Alas, those days were over. For now.

Seth leaned back in his chair. "So there are only four of us left."

No one answered. It was clear that was the case. Seth went on. "Tell me what happened."

Jürgen answered. "The Gargoyles set us up. We knew it would be a setup, but we had made many, many minions and figured we could overpower them. We never expected them to blow up the Parliament."

"You can imagine my surprise"—Seth gestured to the projector screen—"when I turned on the TV and saw the place blown to smithereens."

"The Gargoyles had already destroyed over a third of our minions before the attack and had taken out most of them in the blast. They killed the rest and then tried to dig us up and kill us one by one. They went after Gwen first, but she survived."

"To my dismay." Seth sighed. "Go on."

Jürgen shrugged. "There isn't much more to tell. We were barely hanging on. If the helicopters you sent didn't come when they did, we would be dead."

Seth grinned. "And how about you all say thank you, Seth. You are the most amazing demon ever." He gestured like a conductor.

In unison, they murmured, "Thank you, Seth. You're the most amazing demon ever."

"Oh, it was nothing. I'm glad to help, mainly because we need numbers. Other than Jürgen, I don't care for the rest of you."

James let out a sigh while Gwen rolled her eyes.

Seth stood up and started walking around the table to where Gwen sat. "But I have to wonder, how in the world did you all get tricked?"

Gwen didn't hide the truth. "That hybrid tricked us. We knew he was lying but went in thinking we had the upper hand. It wasn't as if he was successful."

"And yet Darrell is dead. You all would have been dead if it weren't for me. Tell me again how he wasn't successful."

Gwen kept her mouth shut. James didn't blame her.

Jürgen actually spoke up for her. "It wasn't entirely her fault. We would have gone to Parliament that day anyway to turn them all. We never would have imagined that the Gargoyles emptied the building before we were there. The only part that is her fault is making that hybrid who almost killed all of us with his stupid Holy water gun."

James frowned. The next time he saw that hybrid, he was going to rip his head off. James had a feeling that Collin knew to keep his distance now and to not walk around unarmed. He would just not have to do anything rash.

"Well, lucky for you all I have this country under my control. We'll keep an eye out for them if they decide to follow. In the meantime, we'll keep moving forward and head to the Asian continent. Gwen, I know you miss Japan, so the two of you can split off and go there. Jürgen and I can hit up China and Korea."

Gwen grinned. "If you insist. I can't promise how

long it will take though. You know how things go."

"Sure, sure, as long as you're out of my hair and don't die. But first rest here for a week or so. Just in case the Gargoyles are on your tails. We won't let them get the upper hand again."

"Of course." James nodded. "And who knows? Maybe they will slip up and we can take them both out once and for all."

CHAPTER
TWENTY-FOUR

Erik

Erik moaned as he moved his legs off the couch. He had fallen asleep, and when he had awoken, he found that most of the burns were healed, if not at least lessened. His muscles hurt. Maybe he broke more than he originally thought or at least tore some muscles. Or perhaps he was just stiff—he was getting old, after all.

He sat up and felt the room spin a little. How long had he been out? Erik blinked a few times, trying to adjust to the room.

Right. He was in Berlin. They had failed in killing all four demons, but they took one down and didn't let the entire city get destroyed by those two missiles. Granted, a missile of that caliber wouldn't completely demolish, but it would do quite a bit of damage and he didn't want that.

He sighed. Elizabeth, however, was right about them probably going and destroying an entire village out of frustration and hunger. Those lives were on his head now. He felt bad, but he couldn't just watch the scene play out below him. He could hear their screams—he could see the terror in all their faces.

Just like he could in every war.

Erik stood up and found that Elizabeth had gone to sleep in her own bed. Collin was asleep, so perhaps he hadn't slept for a week like he thought he had. He glanced outside to find the sun beginning to rise. Smoke rose in the distance, and he could hear sirens.

So the city was still in chaos. Erik had hoped that it wouldn't be too bad and that the authorities would be able to handle it. Perhaps he was wrong. Humans always had problems with gathering control when chaos ensued. No matter the era, it never changed. That is, as long as they didn't use brute force, although sometimes that even had the opposite effect.

Erik made his way into the kitchenette and opened the fridge. There wasn't anything really inside other than orange juice and some bread and eggs. He decided he could make a small breakfast for everyone for when they awoke, and then they could decide their next move.

Heating up the pan, Erik made the eggs sunny-side up and put the toast in the toaster when Collin stepped out from his room, rubbing his eyes.

"Are you… making breakfast?"

Erik nodded with a little chuckle. "That I am. Hope you like your eggs a little runny."

"I don't care. I just hope I can keep them down. It smells delicious. I haven't had a home-cooked breakfast like this in forever."

Erik had forgotten about that. He just wanted something simple—he wanted to pretend he was just a common human being without having to worry about good versus evil nor about demons trying to destroy the world. He should have known better.

Collin took a seat at the small table. Erik poured him some orange juice and finished up the eggs just as

Elizabeth stepped out of her room. Her hair was a mess and still encrusted in blood. It seemed none of them had cleaned up after their ordeal.

"Good morning, sleepyhead," Erik chimed.

Elizabeth glared at him and took a seat next to Collin. "You do realize that all three of us don't need food, right?"

"I know. I just wanted to do something simple. And besides, it's always nice to have a meal when you need to discuss business."

Elizabeth shrugged. "Whatever."

Erik placed the plate in front of each of them. "Humans do better to discuss their plans around food. Perhaps we should do the same."

Elizabeth took a bite of her toast. Her face softened after she ate a bite. It was true that they didn't need food to sustain life, but good food always helped lift one's spirits.

"So…" Erik cut his egg, and some of the gooey yolk spilled out. "What is our next move?"

Elizabeth kept eating, shaking her head. "I don't know. I really don't know."

"Do you think we should follow the demons?" Collin asked. "I mean, that's the point, right? To defeat them to end this war?"

Erik smiled a little at the boy's suggestion. It was easy to say that when you were just a human who had no idea what the past two thousand years had been like. "They will figure we are coming and have their guard up. We definitely won't be able to sneak attack them or set them up."

"Which means we have practically lost, Erik. We should just... I don't know. Hide? We could hide and they would never get to open the gates to hell."

Collin perked up. "Wait, that's an option? Why haven't you two been doing that this entire time?"

Elizabeth and Erik glanced each other. Elizabeth gestured to him. "You can explain."

Erik sighed. "It's not that simple. First off, we also try to keep the world safe from them and manage any disaster. Second, well, imagine if someone locked themselves in a random room in an apartment complex, but the person trying to find them are sadistic killers who don't care what's destroyed in the process."

"Ah. So they will try to smoke you out," Collin said. "That makes sense."

"Exactly. Imagine though, the entire world is the apartment, and they are making a worse mess of it than this."

Collin raised an eyebrow. "Is that possible?"

"Oh, it is." Elizabeth stabbed an egg with her fork. "Bubonic plague is a great example. The Great Tianqi Explosion. London Smog of 1952. That one church fire in Chile. All the largest disasters that were deemed accidental or from natural causes was from them."

Collin appeared a bit surprised and confused as Erik studied his reaction. Erik went on. "So hiding isn't the easiest thing for us to do. It is why we try to get areas in order and why we follow and try to come up with a plan of attack. Luckily, over the years, we have developed different ways to hide our scent and use our power of persuasion to order attacks against their army, like yesterday."

Nodding, Collin picked at his food. It didn't seem to make him sick, which Erik found to be a good sign. "So we need to wipe them out all at once."

"Or pick them out one by one. I am not sure how that will be possible since they aren't going to want to separate, but it's a strategy," Elizabeth explained.

Collin set down his fork. He seemed to be gathering his thoughts before saying what was on his mind. He let out a breath. "I think I could be used as bait for Gwen.

We could draw her out into the open and then take her out. Once she is out of the picture, then James will be easier to take down. Then the numbers would be even."

Erik eyed him. "You do realize then you will die, right? When Gwen dies, you will."

Collin nodded. "I know, but it would be best to take her out first, right? She is the strongest. And in the process we would be able to take out James as well."

Elizabeth frowned. "In what universe do you think we could corner Gwen, alone, without James? Not to mention they have regrouped and there are four of them."

Collin pointed at himself. "Me. I can take the salt off me, and she will know where I am. I have a feeling, due to her anger and rashness, she will come after me the moment she notices. James will believe it a setup, so either she won't show and we just try something else, or she will sneak away to deal with me herself. Then when she shows, you can destroy her."

Erik had to admit that was a good plan. But whether it would work was another story. "What if she brings everyone? Then you're dead and we'll be down a number."

"It's a chance I'm willing to take. I'll signal if I can

sense them far away or if they are near so you don't have to show your face."

"If they all come," Elizabeth began. "You do realize, they won't just kill you. They will torture you for information. And believe us when we say Gwen knows how to torture physically as well as she can mentally."

Collin nodded slowly. "That is a risk I am willing to take. If it can give you two the advantage, I can do it. It's not like I have any information they can use on you. You both pose no risk."

Erik and Elizabeth glanced at each other. Was this really a good idea? They had put Collin through so much, but he had a point. He was going to lose his life in the end no matter what they did.

Erik gathered the dishes and placed them in the sink. "Well then, I guess we shall head to Moscow as soon as possible."

CHAPTER TWENTY-FIVE

Gwen

Gwen tapped her hand on the table that stood in their hotel room. She didn't like waiting. In fact, waiting was her least favorite thing in the entire world, next to people who talked in theaters. And Holy water. She couldn't forget that horrid liquid.

But waiting was the worst. With waiting, she was left wondering, and wondering made her think of all the things that could go wrong. They could be set aflame again. They could put a bomb under the hotel and evacuate it before James and Gwen even knew, or they could have Russia blown off the map.

Anything was possible now.

It wasn't that the Gargoyles never went to drastic measures, trying to kill them. No, they had rallied troops to stop wars and fight battles before. It was the fact Collin could pinpoint where they were at all times that made her worry. The Gargoyles had a way to shield their smell, but the demons did not. They never had to worry about such things.

She needed to do something about their new weapon. But could she really bring herself to kill Collin? The more she thought about it, the more her gut began to hurt. Why was that, she wondered. Did she truly have feelings for him, or were they just memories of feelings? Either way, it was making her even more uneasy.

"Don't worry, Seth will eventually stop giving you crap. It's only been three days since we got here. He just likes causing drama and being in the center of it," James commented as he took a seat at the table with a beer.

She shook her head. "No, that's not... Huh, you have

a point. He does cause a lot of unneeded drama."

He let out a laugh. "What, are you just figuring that out now?"

Gwen bit at her nail. "I suppose not. I guess I just typically ignored him and didn't pay him much mind. He is always so talkative though. And he did cause a lot of drama in Egypt with all those cats."

James pointed his beer at Gwen. "Exactly. He's still afraid of cats because of that. Or acts like he is. He could just be overdoing it for the attention."

"Maybe we should go gather some cats then. Just for fun."

"I wouldn't say no to that suggestion, but you probably should stay on his good side just in case. Wouldn't want to make him snap and cause another world disaster." James paused and took a swig. "Actually, that might work. Maybe we should."

Gwen chuckled. "He seems to have things all ready to go. If we messed up his plan, we would never hear the end of it no matter where we ended up. Best to play it safe and do as he says."

James took another swig. "Then what's bothering you?"

Gwen hoped he would have forgotten that she had

steered the conversation away from her. She shrugged. "I don't know. Everything? I'm frustrated that Darrell is gone. I'm mad at myself for being such a fool. And I still can't believe they almost killed us all."

He finished up his beer. "I'm going to need another one of these for this conversation, aren't I?"

"Get me one too."

He got up and went into the kitchenette. He grabbed two beers, both pale lagers, and set them on the table. Tossing the bottle opener, James watched as Gwen snatched it out of the air with ease. She opened the bottle and sighed.

"I just don't know, James. What should we do?"

He sat back down and took a swig. "We should go to Japan like Seth wants us to, have fun, go to all the sights you missed, maybe even go to an amusement park. Don't you want to go to an amusement park together? We haven't in the past century."

Gwen did want to. She bit at her nail some more. "But what if they blow it up like last time?"

James sighed. "They aren't going to blow up an amusement park. Are you really paranoid about them now? I haven't known you to ever worry about them."

She took a couple of gulps of her beer. "Well, they

didn't have someone on their team before who could locate where we were."

James didn't comment. He knew that was true. She made a big mistake turning him, and he made the mistake of making her finish the job.

James finally shrugged. "Then we need to kill him. It's that simple."

Gwen frowned and looked away for a second. She knew her mistake when she made it.

"Gwen, dearest, please tell me you want him dead as much as I do."

"I do. I do. I just… I don't know!" She got up and began pacing around. "It's not that I care for him, but my chest hurts. Why does it hurt? Is it because I dated him? Is it because I made him? I want him dead, but why does that make me want to cry, James? I shouldn't want to cry. I like killing things. It's fun."

He sighed as he stood up to face her. "Gwen, look at me in the eyes and promise me you won't do anything stupid again. It took everything I had to not let the others hunt you down and slaughter you. I don't think I can stop them a second time. Besides, Lucifer could show up for a check-in at any time. If you disappoint him, I think he will just take you back down to hell with him."

Gwen let out a breath. He had a good point. It wasn't that she wanted to help the Gargoyles—not after what they had done to her. No, she didn't trust them and didn't believe in them. But was what she was doing the right thing? Or at least the right thing for her?

"I promise I won't betray you again. James, I love you and that will never change. I would fall from Heaven all over again for you. You understand that, right? What happened had nothing to do with you."

He downed the rest of his beer. "Right. I know that. But that doesn't mean it didn't hurt. You know that, right? I felt betrayed, Gwen. You didn't just betray the Twelve, you betrayed me. And I didn't see it coming. I thought I knew you inside and out, but then you went and did that... I just... I just don't know what you're thinking anymore."

Gwen leaned in and kissed him. His mouth taste of beer and blood from the few humans they had devoured hours before at a bar. Gwen backed away.

"I understand that. If you had done what I did to me, I am not sure I could have forgiven you. Although I think I would have found you faster."

James let out a chuckle. "I was giving you some

space."

"Sure. Just admit I am better at tracking someone down."

"Yeah, because you're like a crazy ex-girlfriend."

She laughed. "Isn't that true? But hey, I was able to track down Erik on my own. That should count for something."

James sat down and leaned back. "Yeah, that you did. But he wanted you to find him because of Collin. You would have trouble tracking him now."

He had a point, Gwen knew. The only reason Erik let her come near him was because of Collin. She had no luck trying to find him for decades, and then all of a sudden he showed himself. Gwen frowned.

"Do you think they will show up in Moscow? Or do you think we are going to have to burn them out again?" Gwen asked.

James shrugged. "Who knows? Personally, I hope it's the latter. I would love to cause another disaster. Maybe a new plague? We haven't had one of those in a while."

That made Gwen smile. She did enjoy watching humans be paranoid about something they couldn't see. She grabbed her own beer and finished it. James checked the clock.

"I'm going to go take a shower. In the morning we'll have another meeting. Why the heck Seth likes morning meetings, I have no idea. It's probably just to spite us."

"Probably."

James got up and winked at her. "You may join me, if you want."

She shook her head. "Nah, I got too much on my mind. I'm still sorting it all out."

He paused for a moment, then headed toward the bathroom. "Suit yourself."

Gwen went to the fridge and grabbed another beer. What she really wanted was answers, but none were coming to her. She knew James wouldn't have the answers she needed, as he didn't understand what she was going through. She just couldn't shake off this feeling in her chest.

Did she still love Collin? Even after he betrayed her —even after he almost killed both her and James? And even after him being the reason Darrell was dead?

She felt like she was betraying Darrell more than she was betraying James by trying to sort out her feelings. He was her best friend—they had been through everything together. If anyone knew her as well as James did, it was Darrell. Well, no one could know her as well as James did, but he was a close second.

She popped the top off the beer and took a swig. She had never felt this way before with any minion. Did it have to do with the fact that he couldn't sustain any blood other than her own? Then again, it didn't sound like he had tried human blood, but the Gargoyles' blood should have been enough. What was going on?

Gwen took a deep breath, and that was when she smelled it—Collin was in Moscow. She breathed in again and found that she couldn't sense the Gargoyles. That wasn't a good sign. Was he alone, or were they trying to set her up?

She paced back and forth, debating what to do. James would tell her to leave it alone and wait for Seth to make the decision. His forces, clearly, didn't spot the Gargoyles come into town. Did that mean it really just was Collin? The others would get a scent of him soon, which meant she didn't have much time to act.

Before she could think clearly—and before James could get out of the shower—she grabbed her coat and headed out straight for Collin.

CHAPTER TWENTY-SIX

Collin

Tonight was going to be the night Collin died.

Or at least that was what he believed. In his head, it would either end with them cornering Gwen and killing her, which would also kill him. Or it would end with Gwen or any other demon coming and ripping off his head right then and there. He prayed it was the first one.

He paced back and forth in the alleyway. It was dark and freezing. He didn't think he had ever been so cold in his entire life. Moscow in the late fall was beyond colder than he had ever experienced. It was barely even freezing, but he was used to just wet and cold, not snow and freezing. Ice and snow was already packed down in the area. How many months was it like this here, he wondered. He couldn't imagine what winter was like. He'd rather have the dreary rain of England.

Collin glanced around. Although he couldn't smell them, he knew Erik and Elizabeth were close by, waiting. Once he gave the signal, they would attack. The signal would only be given if he knew she was alone and that none of the other demons would be nearby to save her. The signal being the flare gun he had in his pocket.

It wasn't very discreet, but the Gargoyles decided it was best since they didn't want to be too close in case the other demons showed up. Collin stood on the complete opposite side of Moscow from where he sensed all the demons. He would know if they were getting closer and if the others stayed back.

Time passed as he tried to stay warm. He knew he couldn't get frostbite, per se, but he still felt cold. Hopefully the demons would pick a nice tropical place next time. Collin realized again that there wouldn't be a next time.

His heart began to race. Even though he got to see a lot more than a normal human, he realized he still had a lot he wanted to do before he died. He knew he should count himself lucky as he should have been dead a few years before, but he couldn't stop the thoughts that were now running through his head. He hadn't gotten to go to America or Japan. He wasn't going to be able to see his great-aunt one more time. He would just disappear and his family would never know. He wondered if they even worried about him, other than his great-aunt of course.

Collin shook his head. No, this wasn't the time to have regrets. With his actions he could be saving the world, but it would be a lie to not admit that he didn't feel it was fair that he had to sacrifice himself, and it didn't seem that any other human had ever been in his shoes. Many humans had died, however, because of these battles, so at least he'd gotten to understand why.

Death did not come easy, or at least that was what Collin was figuring out. He wondered if he had lived longer, like the Gargoyles or demons, would he still have regret or be afraid? It always seemed in movies that vampires and immortal creatures were more afraid of death than humans. Was that because they had been hiding for so long they didn't know how to face death? Whereas humans knew it was inevitable and came to accept such things.

He kicked an icy pebble. Why did he have to have such profound thoughts when he should be focusing? Collin took in a deep breath. Gwen had moved closer. She was coming after him. He breathed in again. The others weren't moving. She had snuck away, at least for the time being.

The end was near. Collin could feel his body shaking. Was he going to have enough time to send up the flare? Or was she going to come straight at him, sword in hand, and cut off his head? He gripped the flare and made sure he had it at the ready as she came closer and closer.

Collin could sense every movement she took. She was in a hurry but not as quick as he expected. Perhaps she was trying to make sure no one was following her. The one weakness that the demons had were that they could sense each other, and he could sense them. The only difference in them sensing him was that he could cover himself in Holy water and they no longer could smell him. He was thankful that none of the Holy things burned him. Not only because then he could use it, but also it reminded him that he wasn't a demon but still human with extra abilities.

Now if he could just stop having a need to drink blood, then he would be set.

She was almost upon him. Collin tried not to squeeze the flare gun trigger. That would hurt. At least he would survive, but it would hurt and it would be ever so embarrassing.

Collin didn't like the fact that now his heart felt like it was going to jump out of his chest. It hurt. Was he having a panic attack? Was this why some people mistake panic attacks for heart attacks and vice versa? He didn't have to worry about it being a heart attack since he was practically immortal, but it still hurt.

A figure appeared at the entrance to the alleyway. It was a woman's figure with a red trench coat zipped up and tied with a belt. Her yellow eyes met his gaze as she stuffed her hands in her pockets and walked forward at a moderate pace toward him. He turned to fully face her and waited.

She didn't seem completely angry—he knew this because she wasn't running at him bearing her fangs—but she didn't look like she was in a pleasant mood either. If Collin had to guess, she appeared confused and frustrated. He could relate.

Gwen stopped about three feet away from him, and they simply held each other's stare. Collin pondered on whether he should fire the flare gun now. He had her, and the others were still off in the distance, but something made him want to wait. He needed to know why she'd come if she wasn't going to kill him.

The problem was, she wasn't talking, and he was beginning to feel a bit awkward about it. Did he start the conversation? Should he ask why she showed, as if he didn't know? He was standing in the middle of an abandoned alleyway. If anything looked like a setup, this was it. Yet she still came for a reason, and he was curious as to why that was.

"So...," Collin began, instantly regretting it.

"You killed my best friend," she stated. There didn't seem to be any emotion to that statement as if she was now cold and nothing bothered her any longer.

He looked down. "I'm sorry. I... I don't know what to say since the two of us are on the opposite sides of a war." And it was true. They were, but as they stood there, alone, and she wasn't in her vampire form, he recalled all the dates they had gone on—the nights they cozied up on his couch and drank hot cocoa and watched movies.

"I wish we could go back," he said. It was supposed to be an inner thought, not one he wanted to admit out loud, but there he was, admitting he still loved her. He wanted to punch himself for being such an idiot.

Her eyes darted away, and Collin caught a glimpse of her cheeks turning even pinker than they had been from the cold. "So do I. But realize those had always been lies. That was never the real me."

He shook his head. "No, I disagree. That was the real you and everything else has been fake. You don't like killing. You don't like having to do all this to open the gates of hell. You just do it because you don't have a choice."

She glared at him—her eyes flashing yellow. "Don't you dare say that. You have no idea what I have been through. You have no idea what I am thinking and what I want."

"But I see your eyes, and I know when you kill that you have a little bit of sadness. I get it, Gwen. I know what it's like to struggle between good and evil."

She shook her head. "No, you don't. You have no idea the difference between good and evil. You just know good and evil from church, but you don't know what we demons have gone through—you don't know what was done to us in Heaven. And you don't comprehend the difference in treatment between us and you humans. Humans can seek redemption. When they do something bad and want to apologize, they are forgiven—they can turn their lives around and do good and be redeemed. Not for us though. Once we turned, we were never given the chance to turn back. We have to live with guilt, and we can't do anything or else we are tortured for an eternity. It is the opposite for humans; they are given paradise."

Collin frowned. He never thought of it that way. "Would you undo what you did to go back to Heaven? Didn't you say the reason you were cast out of Heaven was so you could be with James? Would you take that back so you could be with him again?"

"No, I don't think I could. But that's the other unfair thing about all this. Humans are capable of being with each other, and we Angels are not. You lot have been given everything, and you squander it, not realizing how blessed you truly are."

Collin had no response for that. She was right; that didn't seem fair. But he didn't know what Heaven was like—he didn't know what it was like being an Angel and given strict rules.

Gwen went on. "That is why we demons hate humans so much and want to watch them suffer. We know that you will be forgiven and be given whatever you want. We hate it."

"So demons are just envious?"

She smiled. "It's one of the deadly sins. Us demons love all seven equally though."

"So why did you decide to come here, Gwen? Did you just want to tell me how it's unfair that I am a human and you're not?"

She shrugged. "I don't know. I don't know anything anymore. I don't know what I want. I don't know how I can keep going. I don't have a choice in anything, but I know I can't turn my back on James. I just can't—" Gwen stopped, her eyes starting to tear up.

Collin couldn't believe what he was hearing. After everything, was she still having second guesses? Could she turn to their side again and help them? Collin took his hand out of his pocket and touched her hands. "What do you want, Gwen? Tell me what you want to do, and I'll help you."

CHAPTER TWENTY-SEVEN

James

James stepped out of the shower and found Gwen to be long gone. He took a few deep breaths, trying to center himself before he went after her and stopped her from making a huge mistake. He took in one last large breath and found that Collin was letting them sense where he was. It was more than likely a setup, and if he wasn't quick, she could lose her life.

As he grabbed his phone, he saw that Jürgen was trying to call. That was not what he needed. Jürgen didn't ever call for a friendly chat. It had to be urgent. It was probably about Collin.

"What?" James answered with a grunt.

"Come to the meeting room. We have a visitor."

James felt as if his heart had sunk into his stomach and his entire body had turned into ice. It couldn't be possible—the timing couldn't be any worse. "Lucifer is here."

"Yup, and he wants to speak to all of us, including Gwen."

James gulped. "Gwen kind of ran off."

"Oh, I know. I sensed her move the moment I sensed Collin. So call her and tell her to get her ass back here or else there is going to be hell to pay."

"I'll go and—" James began, but Jürgen cut him off.

"No, you aren't going to risk that. Call her, and if she doesn't answer, then that is her own Goddamn fault. She will pay the price for not listening, but if you go and you both get yourself killed, then Lucifer will have a very special spot for you the moment you appear in hell. I can guarantee you, it won't be pleasant."

James hung up the phone. He would do as Jürgen asked because he was right—he didn't want to die and have to deal with his special spot in hell.

Quickly he clicked on Gwen's number. As it rang, he heard buzzing coming from the table. He cursed under his breath. Of course she didn't take her phone. Shaking his head, he grabbed his coat and headed toward the meeting room.

The building that Seth had acquired was two blocks from the hotel Gwen and James were staying. With his superspeed, he was there in under a minute. He took a deep breath and entered the building. Once he got inside the elevator, he could sense him—the Devil himself. It had been a century since James had felt his presence. The aura that filled the building was cold—colder that the worse storm in all of Russia. James would know; he'd been in that storm. This was a different feeling of cold like no other. It was like the absence of anything warm, and yet he was light itself. It was a sick joke, James felt, as there was nothing light about him, in that Christians believed all things in light were good. That was where they were wrong, as Lucifer meant light-bringer. It was ironic really.

The elevator doors opened, and James mentally

prepared himself for the scolding of a century. He kept one part of his mind on Gwen, however, and tried to make sure she was all right. So far she was still alive, and he didn't smell any blood. The Gargoyles would have another thing coming if they realized Lucifer was there. Although he couldn't kill anyone, he could cause a lot of damage if he wanted. He typically didn't as that was James's job, and he just came to check in and make sure they remembered who they served.

Yeah, he was going to get a big scolding for what Gwen had done, especially since she wasn't there to release his anger on.

Stupid, stupid Gwen. Why did Collin have to reveal himself at the exact same moment? James was going to have to punish Gwen or else the others would. With a sigh, he stepped inside the meeting room.

A man wearing a fancy black Victorian-style coat, like something a vampire in a cheesy movie would wear, stood in the meeting room. His hair was pulled back in a similar Victorian fashion. He had appeared that way since the 1800s. It was apparent that he liked that era and its style. James had to admit, he did miss the era, although mainly because the smog in the cities was so thick that he and Gwen could cause as much trouble as they wanted and no one saw.

"James, it's a pleasure to see you again." He glanced behind him, as if he didn't know Gwen wasn't with him. "Where is the lovely Gwen?"

James bit his tongue and took a deep breath before answering, "She's preoccupied."

Lucifer raised an eyebrow. "Oh? With something more important than me?"

"She didn't know you were coming and ran off without her phone."

James glanced at Seth and Jürgen who weren't going to come to his rescue anytime soon. They wanted to see Lucifer take out his frustrations on the two of them. Great.

"And here I thought you told Seth and Jürgen that you had everything under control. Apparently you were mistaken." Lucifer walked around the table to where James stood.

"She's fine. We had a whole discussion about it."

"Before she ran off again."

"With all due respect, my Lord, she didn't run off. She is simply dealing with an issue."

Lucifer smacked James across the face with the back of his hand. Lucifer, of course, wore rings with large jewels on them. Was that because he liked how they looked or to make his slaps hurt more? James wasn't sure. All he knew was that it hurt. A lot.

"Ow." James touched his burning face to find that the gems did, in fact, cut him.

Lucifer licked the blood off his rings. "You may take a seat. We have a lot to go over."

James took a seat but not without shooting a glare at Jürgen and Seth, who were chuckling.

"Now, where was I before James waltzed in?" Lucifer asked.

"You were talking about how we all would be boiled alive for a century if we failed this mission."

Lucifer grinned. "That's right. Thank you. Boiled alive for a century, then some nice skewers while hanging by one's toe for another century, and I have a feeling after that, I'll have many more surprises. Who knows? I can get pretty creative in hell. I get some pretty high ratings by all the souls that are stuck there."

"But you're keeping the best for us, right sir?" James sarcastically commented.

"Of course. And I have a very special room for you and Gwen. Don't worry, you will still be together for an eternity like I promised but mainly so you can watch each other suffer."

James made a small grimace. At least he would be keeping his word, but being tortured like that for an eternity did not sound pleasant. He was a masochist, yes, but only to an extent and mainly only for Gwen.

He was pissed at her for disappearing. He could still sense she was fine, but she wasn't going to be fine for long once Lucifer was done with this meeting—at least that's what he expected.

"Now, the great thing is, you don't have to worry about suffering for an eternity if you just do your Goddamn jobs! Kill those Gargoyles and then eternal bliss. Whatever you want, it's yours. You can find a nice island, stay there for all I care. Just open that gate."

Easier said than done. They had been trying to open it for two thousand years. James didn't even know if it was possible. What if it had been a lie? What if they killed the last two Gargoyles and there was something else they would have to do too? James didn't know if he could take much more of this. Lucifer said that the end would be when they killed the Son of God. That clearly didn't work.

"Don't worry, Your Majesty." Seth kissed Lucifer's ass. "I am in charge this round, and I won't let anyone mess up. Not even Gwen."

"And yet she isn't here. Swell job you're doing."

Seth frowned and shot James daggers. James simply shrugged.

Oh yeah, Gwen was definitely going to be in trouble. Big time. Who exactly was going to deal out the punishment was up for grabs, but he hoped they all got to take a crack at her.

"Now, do you have plans for taking out the Gargoyles?" Lucifer asked.

James leaned back and let Seth answer. He was going to get scolded. James was enjoying this even if he got slapped in the face with razor-sharp rings.

"Well, first we have to locate them," Seth began. Jürgen and James exchanged glances. "And then we are going to go corner them."

Lucifer stared at Seth. "That's it?"

Seth scrambled with the papers. "Well, I mean… We are going to split up and take over China, Japan, and the rest of Asia. The Gargoyles are short on numbers and will mess up, and we'll be there to take them down."

"Take them down, eh? Like you did in Berlin? Oh wait, no. You lost Darrell in that attack. Explain to me how that happened."

Seth started stuttering, not sure how to respond. "Well, you see, I, um…" His eyes darted toward James. He pointed his finger. "Gwen's hybrid tricked us. If she hadn't gotten that human involved, the war would have been over."

Lucifer let out a sigh. "If Gwen did what she was told many times, this war would have been over. But that doesn't matter, I'll deal with her on my own. But you have authority over everyone. Use it."

"I will, sir. Don't worry. Once she is back, I'll make sure she knows her place."

"She will know her place when she gets back here because I'll first go and have a talk with her." Lucifer smiled. "But you can deal out any punishment you see fit, just to make sure."

James gulped. He feared for Gwen, but it really had been her fault. She shouldn't have run off on her own.

"I most definitely will punish her when she gets back." Seth grinned. "You can count on that."

Lucifer turned to James. "And James, if you don't keep a handle on your girl, you two will regret ever disappointing me."

James sarcastically grinned. "Don't worry. I heard you the first time."

With that, Lucifer disappeared to go find Gwen.

James closed his eyes, trying to calm himself down. "Damn it, Guinevere."

CHAPTER TWENTY-EIGHT

Erik

Erik didn't like how long it was taking for Collin to use the flare gun. If he didn't ignite it, it meant one of three things: Gwen never showed, Gwen killed him before he could use it, or the others showed and it was a failed mission. He hoped it was the first of those three. He didn't want Collin to die even though he knew in the end that might happen.

"Ugh, what is taking him so long?" Erik whispered to

Elizabeth. They were a few blocks away—far enough not to be spotted by the demons but close enough that they could get to Collin quicklyif the trap had worked.

"Give him some time. She might be wary of it."

"But then she would alert the others and he could be dead."

She didn't answer because she knew he was right. Erik let out another sigh and waited. It was all they could do. If Collin was fine, he would simply come to where they were waiting, and if he wasn't fine, well, then they would have to figure out if they'd taken him or if he was dead. Gwen would make a scene if she killed him, so at least they would be able to find his body. Hopefully.

Elizabeth stayed still, taking deep, long breaths to calm herself. This could be just another failed mission, and they would be outnumbered two to one. Erik didn't like those odds—especially since he didn't feel either of them could take on Gwen and James together. The only way they could was through that explosion, just like Elizabeth planned, but even that had failed. The demons were lucky, and they knew that. Now they were going to be extra careful. At least that's what Erik believed.

"She's probably not stupid enough to come out here

alone. They will think it's a trap and leave him alone. He will probably show his head around here in a bit," Elizabeth commented. "I mean, I wouldn't show up after what all we did to them."

Erik squatted down to stretch his legs a little. "Here's the thing. Gwen doesn't think before she acts if she is angry or upset. So she might want to talk to Collin, or kill him, after everything that happened. He is her creation after all; she won't be able to resist the temptation."

Elizabeth glanced at Erik from the corner of her eye. "What, are you an expert on all things Gwen now?"

He shrugged. "She and I go way back. I've watched her. I've experienced many, many horrible things by her hand, but I have also seen her try to repent. She doesn't really make sense, but I can tell you one thing. She acts straight on emotion."

"You really think that wasn't part of some act? You think she was actually wanting to repent?"

"I think she had some doubts. But as we have said, the demons can't repent for what they did. They turned their backs on God and went with Lucifer. There is no coming back from that."

Elizabeth looked out on the city from the roof they

stood on. "Humans get to. That was probably why she tried. Maybe she did think it was possible."

Erik agreed that the fact that the humans got to repent while demons could not didn't seem fair, but it wasn't up to them—it was up to God Himself. What happened during the war was not the same as what humans faced or knew. Humans didn't know for a fact that God existed, whereas demons, when they were Angels, did. But they still betrayed Him, and that was why they were banished.

"I wonder if they would still pick Lucifer, knowing what they now know," Erik pondered. "Would they still go through all that torment for the lie that was freedom? They should know by now there was no such thing as freedom. All of it was a lie. They are less free than they had ever been."

"Honestly, Erik, I think they would still do it. Lucifer is cunning in his lies. He would make them pick him all over again. Even Gwen would because she fell for something selfless."

"You think love is selfless? In the way they love?"

"I think she picks James over loving anything else, including God. That was the problem, and that was why she fell."

Erik paused for a brief moment. She must have made a point and made it well. Erik never had loved someone else—no one ever had. It was only Gwen and James who had fallen in love, and they even performed a blood bond that would leave them connected forever. There weren't many who would sacrifice themselves like that so that they could be with the one they loved.

"I still think they would be stupid to pick falling from Heaven all over again. To be damned to this world and then hell if they fail?"

"Aren't we stuck on this world as well? Having to face their wrath?"

Erik chuckled. "Fair point. But when we die, we go back to Heaven. If they die, they will go to hell to be tortured for an eternity."

"So what you're saying is that they have more to lose and will fight to the end. Great."

She had another good point. They would fight harder not because it was what they believed to be right, but because they didn't want to face the consequences of losing. Although God would be disappointed in them, he would know that they did what they could, and they would go on. As for Gwen and the others, they were facing eternal torture. He promised them freedom by just disobeying God, but that freedom was a lie. He kept asking more and more of them with the promise they could do anything. It seemed to him they had more restraints than when they were in Heaven. Except for love, that is.

"Maybe she is going to be a no-show," Elizabeth said. "I think we would have heard something otherwise if it all went to hell."

Erik was about to agree when he felt something in the air shift. It was as if he had been thrown in space where there was an absence of everything warm. He quickly glanced over at Elizabeth, who had the same worried look on her face.

"That can't be. Has it really been a century?" Elizabeth asked.

Clearly it had. Lucifer was in the city. Erik took a deep breath and let it out slowly. He couldn't fight in the war. He couldn't hurt them, but that didn't mean either of them wanted to go near him. He was the one who had caused all this; he was the one who'd made a mess of everything. All because of his pride.

"Erik, I know he can't fight us, but he can hurt the demons, correct?"

Erik nodded. "Yeah, he usually comes to threaten

them and give them a morale boost, so to speak."

"What about hybrids?"

Erik felt as if reality just smacked him on the side of the face. Could he touch hybrids? Could he do something to Collin?

No, this wasn't good. What if Gwen went to see Collin and Lucifer did too? What if Collin believed that creature's lies and deceit? Humans had no chance against the power that carried with his voice. It was a good thing that he could only appear once a century, as he had caused many problems in the past by convincing humans to follow him. It was only a brief moment, almost like he plants a seed and later those humans would go on to do terrible things.

"He will be fine. Lucifer is probably with the rest of the demons, discussing how they are going to brutally massacre us. They probably completely forgot about Collin."

Elizabeth gave him a look.

"Yeah, I know. I'm lying out my teeth. I'm just trying to convince myself that it will be fine."

But it wouldn't be fine. They couldn't exactly come to his aid, as they didn't want to make the situation worse. Erik prayed—he prayed hard that someone would save Collin or that they did, in fact, forget about him. He closed his eyes and took a deep breath.

Please… God…

CHAPTER TWENTY-NINE

Gwen

He believed her.

Gwen tried not to smile. This human hybrid believed her. She had made him watch her massacre people—made him give her information in exchange for killing a human for him. And he believed her when she acted like she still had doubts.

Pathetic. Gwen wanted to berate him for believing in what a demon would say. She warned him time and time again how she was not human and that he couldn't change her mind no matter how hard he tried.

She clutched his hands. "I just… I don't want to go on with opening the gates of hell. Lucifer says he will give us freedom then, but he also said he was going to give us freedom once we destroyed the Son of God, and that clearly didn't happen. I just… I don't know what to do."

Gwen tried her best to sound convincing. She knew if any of the demons heard her, they would think she was betraying them. She sensed all the others were back at the hotel or in the business building. They were nowhere near her.

So what was her plan now? Well, that was simple. She was going to trick Collin into letting her see Elizabeth and Erik. Not right away but at a later date. Then the demons would ambush them and take down at least one more Gargoyle. Seth was going to be mad that she took the initiative, but she had to. She had to see what Collin was going to do.

And he was going to betray her. She could see it in his eyes. He wanted her to appear here alone and was going to signal the Gargoyles to try to take her out. She could make out the flare gun in his pocket.

Gwen pushed back the anger. She would get her revenge—she would use him and then he would understand the pain of losing a friend and being betrayed by someone you once loved.

"You want to help the Gargoyles?"

She nodded with a sniffle. "I want to end this war. I want to finally be rid of this curse."

Collin didn't say anything for a moment. If he had half a brain, he would have fired that flare gun the moment he'd seen her.

"You are willing to die for that? Because you would have to die, you know that, right?"

"If I die, so would you. Are you willing to give up your life as well?"

Collin slowly nodded. "I am."

"Then let me settle things with the others. Let me sabotage their plans and meet you. Then I'll surrender and the Gargoyles can destroy me once and for all. James will then be easy to take down, and I can give Elizabeth and Erik all the info they need to take down the other two."

Gwen knew that sounded too good to be true. But Collin still watched her, as if trying to figure out if she was being honest.

"Why would you do that?"

She let out a sigh. "Because, during our last fight when I was so close to death, I realized that it was what I truly wanted—I wanted to die. It was why I fell for your ruse. I subconsciously wanted it all to end."

"I guess that—" Collin stopped and turned. "What's that feeling?"

Gwen should have noticed earlier. She took in a breath and realized he was here. It was as cold as being locked in a freezer, which had happened once or twice. But at the same time, his scent was perfect. It was light; it was something that couldn't compare to anything else. Yet it made her sick with the memories of everything he had done to her—and made her do.

"Collin. Run," she ordered, and she turned toward the scent, trying to figure out where he was going to come from.

Collin just stood there, ignoring the request. "But we haven't finished—"

Gwen turned to face him. "I said run!"

She shoved him back, but she already knew it was too late. His presence filled the air, bringing a slight chill that even a demon like her couldn't ignore. Turning around, she faced him. He smiled with his perfect, chiseled jaw. His dark hair was pulled back, and he wore a Victorian-style jacket. It was strange and yet fit him well. His eyes shone like the moon as they studied her with dark intent. Anyone who saw him would think he was an Angel, and they wouldn't be far off.

"Lucifer," Gwen whispered with a gulp. She saw Collin freeze in the corner of her eye.

"Gwen, my child, it has been a while." He licked his gentle lips as he examined Collin. "I see you have been causing some trouble for my generals."

"He's nothing I can't handle." She held her head high. If she showed any weakness, he would pounce on it in a second.

"Really? Then explain to me why Darrell is in hell with the others."

Gwen fidgeted with her sleeve. "It was an accident. It should have been me."

"And dearest, I wish it were. You wouldn't believe what I have planned for you for messing all this up. This world should have been mine already if it weren't for you and your stupid little conscience."

"Don't worry. I'm back now. I'll bring this world down for you. Nothing will stop me."

"Really?" Lucifer turned to Collin. "Not even this human whom you so desperately had to keep alive?"

Gwen hesitated. "No."

Lucifer's lips curled into a smile as he stepped toward Collin. Collin tried to back away but was cornered by the wall. His face was white, stricken by the being that stood before him. Lucifer, Satan, the Devil, in human form, standing in front of him. Every human's worst nightmare come to life. He was the one who could take you to hell and never let you out. The prince of lies, the morning star, the most powerful cherub in the Heavens. He wasn't a creature you wanted to face even if you were a demon.

"Collin, isn't it?" he whispered softly.

Collin nodded. "Yes."

"You have any idea what Gwen did to you?"

"She brought me back to life."

Lucifer chuckled. "If it were merely that simple. She went against my strict orders to never bring a human back to life. She has given you her strength, leaving you at an advantage against her. A human shouldn't have that strength. Humans are just lost sheep to be preyed upon. You understand?"

Collin didn't say a word. Gwen wanted Lucifer out of

there. He was destroying her plan to set up the Gargoyles. They had to know he was there—even Gargoyles could sense Lucifer's presence.

"But you're no longer that sheep; she made you into a wolf. A wolf that can help destroy the sheep. You can help us, Collin. You can help destroy this planet and bring hell to Earth."

"Why would I do that?"

Lucifer grabbed Collin by the back of his neck and steadied his gaze. "Because I can give you anything you desire. This new world I'll create, you can have anything you want. Land, riches, women, you name it. It will all be yours. And the fear in your heart that you will go to hell for helping me, it will never happen. Hell will no longer exist, and you will spend eternity however you please."

Gwen watched as Collin's eyes became glossy. He had him under his spell. While it would be beneficial to have Collin on their side, Gwen wanted him to help her betray the Gargoyles—she wanted to watch his face as she betrayed him and slaughtered Elizabeth. And there was only one way to convince Collin she wanted to help him. She was going to regret it, however, as Lucifer didn't appreciate anyone interfering with what he wanted to do.

"Stop it!" she cried out, but they both ignored her.

"All you have to do, Collin, is to sacrifice your blood to me." Lucifer slowly moved his mouth toward his neck.

Knowing she would regret it later, Gwen grabbed Lucifer and pulled him back. "Collin, snap out of it and get out of here!"

Collin shook his head and saw what happened. He didn't hesitate to leave the place at once.

Instead of the beating she presumed would come, Lucifer just laughed. "This makes things more interesting."

Gwen let go of Lucifer and backed up a few steps. "What do you mean?"

"You still feel for that human, yet James loves you more than life itself. He would give everything to make sure you're safe, yet you would sacrifice yourself for another man. What would he say if he knew that?"

Gwen glanced back at where Collin once stood. "That's not it. I have a plan."

He raised an eyebrow. "A plan? Really? Well, I can tell you now that the others don't know of any plan. Either you're lying to me or you're acting on your own again, which I also dislike."

"It was a spur-of-the-moment plan. I should have waited, but…"

"But you like acting out of instinct? Or did you decide on the plan after you saw your human lover's face and you decided you couldn't kill him?"

Tears began to fill her eyes. Perhaps he hit the nail on the head. "Why are you here?"

"You sound angry. Is that really a way to greet your master?"

"Sorry," she replied. "Why does thou greet us with your presence, Your Highness?" She made a curtsy.

"I'll pretend I don't hear the sarcasm in that question. I have come to see how my generals are doing. I didn't expect to lose another, not when the end is so close."

"It won't happen again. I plan to tear that Gargoyle limb from limb. The plan is already set in stone. That is until you showed up."

"Are you trying to get on my bad side, Gwen? Because you're doing a fantastic job at it."

"Aren't I already on your bad side?"

He grinned. "No matter how much you piss me off, you always make me smile. Perhaps it's because I can imagine exactly what I am going to do to you and

James if you fail."

Gwen frowned. She knew he wasn't jesting—threats were never lies.

He went on. "But that still leaves the problem of Collin…"

"I said I can handle him."

Hot pain engulfed the side of her face as he slapped her. He always wore sharp rings.

"Liar! He has caused enough trouble for me. Deal with him or I'll have the others deal with him as they please."

"Yes, sir."

"And Gwen?"

She looked back at him. He had a wide smile sprawled across his face.

"These bodies grow tiresome so fast. You stopped my chance to feed."

Gwen slowly moved her coat collar away from her neck, half regretting stopping him from feeding on Collin now. The aftereffects of his bite weren't ones she wanted to deal with right then. She would also have to explain to James why he had fed on her, and he would hate her for letting Collin slip away. She shut her eyes tightly as his fangs pierced her neck, a cold chill running through her body, as if death was at her throat.

CHAPTER THIRTY

Collin

Collin ran as fast as he could. He didn't know which way he was heading and whether or not it was back toward the rendezvous point, but he didn't care at the moment. He just needed to get out of there, and any direction would do.

What that was, Collin wasn't sure. He understood it was Lucifer, but at the same time couldn't comprehend what scene he had left. The Prince of Darkness himself was trying to drag Collin down to hell. Collin had never felt anything so cold and dark and yet so bright and beautiful at the same time. He was completely taken by surprise. Never in his wildest dreams would he imagine he would come face-to-face with the Devil and for him to be that beautiful.

Granted, the style he was wearing had been outdated for two centuries. The man, or Angel or whatever, could pull it off. It was the least part about him that stuck out, as the rest of him was utterly bright and beautiful and yet dark. Collin didn't know how to put it in his own thoughts, as he had never witnessed something so fantastic and terrifying at the same time.

His heart felt like it could jump out of his chest. He was beginning to understand Gwen better now. He could see why she had done all the things she had as a demon—there was no saying no to that… thing.

Collin stopped and turned to look back from the direction he ran. Gwen had stood up to Lucifer to save him. She could have let Lucifer have his way with him, but instead, she risked her life to help him run away. Perhaps she was telling the truth. Perhaps she really did want to help the Gargoyles by getting information and sacrificing herself.

He felt like a naive idiot for believing her, but after seeing what she did, and who she stood up against, what if she was telling the truth? What if she really wanted to sacrifice herself?

It was a huge risk to trust her, but something in his heart wanted to believe her. That, however, was what differentiated humans from demons. Collin knew he had a heart and that she, in a way, did not. There was no redemption for her; there was no reason for her to feel remorse.

But she had stood up to Lucifer.

He didn't know what to do. First of all, he needed to get back to the Gargoyles and report what had happened. They weren't going to like the fact that he'd had the chance to take Gwen out and he didn't take it. He might have cost them the war. He shook his head. No, there were a lot of variables. Besides, Lucifer had shown up. Collin had a feeling that would have ruined everything if they had tried to kill her.

Collin headed toward the rendezvous point. He just hoped they were still there, though he figured if they weren't, then they would be back at the hotel. Collin pulled his coat tighter, the cold, Russian air getting to him after he stopped running. Now he knew what was even colder than this place—Lucifer himself.

He shuddered at the thought of Lucifer. He didn't want to ever have to face him again. Collin felt his mind drift when Lucifer spoke—it was as if his words were laced with sweetness and almost some sort of high. Collin hadn't done drugs since high school, and that was just some weed that a friend had stolen from his older brother. No, it was different than that—almost like complete bliss. Which made it all the more terrifying.

Collin felt like he was going to have another panic attack. Taking a few deep breaths, he somewhat regained his senses. But that didn't stop him from wanting to cry and run and never look back. He had seen demons, fought them, and fought the creatures they created, but he knew he had no chance against that. Nothing could have prepared him for *that*.

The rendezvous point wasn't far from where he ran, which was a blessing. His body wanted to collapse as soon as possible. The hotel was on the other side of Moscow, unfortunately, but at least he could rest in the cab they would grab. First he just had to cover himself in Holy water so Gwen and the others couldn't sense where he was going.

Erik was waiting for him. Collin could tell he was anxious as there was a line where he walked back and forth in the snow. The moment Erik saw him, relief filled his eyes.

"Oh, Collin, thank the Heavens. I was worried… I sensed…," Erik began.

"Lucifer? Yeah, I was there when he showed up."

Erik's eyes widened. "You… How?"

Collin scratched the back of his head. "Yeah, I'll explain later. Can we get out of here? I feel like I'm going to pass out."

Erik nodded as they headed to a major road as Collin sprayed himself down and waved for a taxi. Or at least a car that would take them to the hotel. While there were taxi companies in Moscow, anyone could stop to pick up a passenger and charge them to take them across town. It was terrifying, and if it weren't for the fact that Collin was a hybrid, he would not get in a random person's car there. Or anywhere, for that matter. The world was a terrifying place for that much trust in a stranger.

A car stopped and Erik offered five hundred rubies. The man agreed, and they got in the back of the blue Hyundai Solaris. The inside smelled of cigarette smoke, which made Collin's nose crinkle. At least it wasn't the smell of blood, but still. He hated cigarette smoke. It reminded him too much of his father and mother.

Collin sighed as he stared out the window of the car. Moscow was a rather beautiful city with a mixture of modern buildings and old architecture of the Orthodox churches and the old, almost gothic styles. It was quite a different mix, but beautiful nevertheless. He took in a deep breath, and through the smoke he could sense James. He was going to retrieve Gwen. Collin wondered what was taking him so long and if he knew Lucifer had gone after her. It would make sense if Lucifer didn't want to be interrupted, especially since Collin had his suspicion that Lucifer could sense Collin. It had been a close one and definitely wasn't on his list of things that could have gone wrong.

Gwen had definitely been bitten. He smelled her blood as he'd run away. He felt bad, but he couldn't do anything to save her. He knew he was outmatched, and if he tried anything, Lucifer could take him to hell. That was not something Collin ever wanted to experience. He also came close to Lucifer biting his neck, of which Collin didn't know what would have happened then. What would it have felt like? He had his suspicion that it wasn't a pleasant experience.

Lucifer had offered more power. Collin wasn't sure if that was something he had ever wanted. It wasn't like when he was growing up he wanted power or to be strong, or at least not intentionally. Perhaps, after dealing with his entire family mentally and emotionally abusing him and his father coming home drunk more nights than not, that he wanted to be strong and show them who was in control. Or perhaps deep down every human wanted power one way or another. Or perhaps Lucifer could convince anyone to want anything because he had a way of speaking.

It wasn't power that Collin wanted but freedom to control his life. He didn't want what Lucifer offered because in the end he wouldn't be free. Gwen, however, didn't have freedom and believed his lies. Now that she was stuck doing his bidding for centuries, perhaps she was telling the truth about wanting to help him. If they were promised freedom and yet had been working for him for so long, he could understand resenting everything and wanting to make a difference.

Which was why he chose to believe her.

They arrived at the hotel, and Erik paid the driver. The man waved and drove off to either pick up more people or call it a night. Erik and Collin went up to their room to find Elizabeth rocking back and forth on the couch. She quickly stood up when she saw them step in.

"Why didn't you text me that he showed up?" she asked Erik.

Erik scratched the back of his head. "Oops, sorry about that. I was so relieved he finally showed up that I completely forgot."

She rolled her eyes. "Whatever. What happened, Collin? Start from the beginning."

Collin sat down, not sure where to start. He shook his head. "I don't know. I'm just... really tired. Can I rest for a bit and then we talk? I need to gather my thoughts."

She studied him for a second, then nodded. "Of course."

He got up and went into his room. He felt like a jerk as they had been worried about him, but he really did need some rest before going into what had happened, and he needed all his mental strength to convince them to trust Gwen and let him try to make her come out one more time.

Collapsing onto his bed, he passed out in mere seconds.

CHAPTER
THIRTY-ONE

James

James sat in the office chair, twirling around and around, debating if he should go after Gwen or not. It was her own damn fault for following Collin without telling him, but he was afraid of what Lucifer might do to her.

At least he didn't have to worry about the Gargoyles killing her. He just had to worry about how much Lucifer was going to hurt her. It wouldn't be just enough to take her back to hell with him, so at least there was that. But if he took her blood, she was going to be suffering the effects for days.

"You're making me sick, watching you. Could you please stop spinning?" Seth commented.

James spun one more time and then stopped. He leaned back and stared up at the ceiling.

Jürgen tapped his finger on the table. "It's her own fault, you know."

"Oh, I know."

"She always makes you worry, and yet you still love her."

"That I do."

"Even though she fell for that hybrid. I say we just kill him."

James turned to Jürgen. "We should. Right now. Let's go."

Seth held out his hand. "Wait. No. If Lucifer is there, he will handle him. If Collin already ran off, then he would be with the Gargoyles, and I am not dealing with losing the two of you."

Both James and Jürgen slumped back into their chairs, groaning.

"Don't worry. We'll take him out soon. And Gwen

better come up with a convincing story as to why she ran off without us," Seth added.

James agreed. He wanted to say it wasn't like her to do such a thing, but he was finding that was a lie. She acted on her emotions—it was why they fell from Heaven, after all. But he wasn't appreciating her keeping him out of the loop this time around. He thought he meant more than that.

Perhaps she didn't betray him this time. Perhaps she went to cut that hybrid's head off and serve it to him on a golden platter just like she promised. He knew that probably wasn't the case, but he could hope.

He checked the clock. How much time had it been? How much time should he wait until he could go out there and help her? He didn't want to piss off Lucifer, and he didn't want to trigger a trap for him and Gwen.

Ugh, where is she?

"Calm down, James. I can feel the tension coming off you like a wave of Holy water. It's making me uneasy," Seth commented.

James slammed his fist on the table. "Shut up, Seth! I don't care you don't like my tension! I'm pissed off!"

Jürgen slapped the table. "And whose fault is that? You are the one who decided to perform a blood bond with that wench!"

He glared at Jürgen. "What is your two's problem? You used to get along, and then all of a sudden you have been cold to her."

"Because she betrayed our kind!"

James shook his head. "No, before that. You have been giving her crap and the cold shoulder way before then. What the heck happened to you two?"

Jürgen stood and leaned forward on the table. "Because your fucking bitch of a lover killed my wife!"

James glanced over at Seth, who was also perplexed. James turned back to him and slowly opened his mouth. "What?"

Slamming his fist on the table, Jürgen went on. "I made a hybrid. She was a countess in Hungary when I was living it up in Eastern Europe. I loved her—she was the only person I had ever loved. We had made a pact not to make a hybrid centuries before, but I was going to do it as her bloodlust was as great as a demon's and she wasn't even turned yet."

James didn't like where this was going. How did he not know about this? He was probably there? Did Jürgen keep this a secret from them? Did he have a human lover? That wasn't someone he was just going to toss aside?

"Her name was Elizabeth Bathory. I promised her the world—I promised her an eternity with us."

Seth crossed his arms. "We promised no more hybrids."

"Yeah. We did. And yet pretty little Gwen gets her way and makes her human lover into one. She already had you, James! And yet my wife was ripped to shreds by that very person. Does that seem fair?"

He didn't know how to respond. Had he known, would he have stopped Gwen? James was right. They had promised no more hybrids, but Gwen had made one. She made one after killing Jürgen's. And she was the one who wanted redemption? It didn't make sense. She had done many dark and sadistic things but not typical against other demons. There had to be something else to it.

James got up and left the conference room. He needed to talk to Gwen. He needed to know what was going through her mind right that instant.

When he stepped outside, he took a deep breath. He could smell her blood in the distance. So Lucifer had drunk from her before he returned to Hell. Great. He took another breath and found that Collin was quite a ways away from her. That meant he wouldn't have to worry about the Gargoyles attacking him. Probably.

He didn't like the fact that Collin could pinpoint their location. It wasn't something they were used to worrying about. Granted, they left a trail of blood wherever they went, and the Gargoyles easily followed that. This was a bit different. The only reason that hybrid was still alive was because he had the protection of those Gargoyles. They had hoped that Collin would betray the Gargoyles because of his lust for blood, but they were greatly mistaken. He was loyal to them even though he craved blood. This hybrid wasn't like any of the others. This made James wonder what Jürgen's wife could have been like. Maybe she wouldn't have gone crazy and disobeyed them—causing more bloodshed than even those demons. But, by the sounds of it, she was already a bit crazy.

James used his speed to make his way through the city. He didn't want to leave Gwen as vulnerable as she was alone. If the Gargoyles figured out what had happened, they might have gone after her to finish the deal. She wouldn't have been able to put up any sort of fight, which meant she would have to sit and listen to him scold her.

Not that that would do anything. Gwen didn't really listen when she was scolded, which made her just do whatever it was over again. She had problems with authority, to say the least. James did his best to listen to Lucifer and not talk back, but he had a feeling Gwen talked back to Lucifer. It would be the only reason he would have let Collin go and not bring him to his side.

Most humans didn't stand a chance. Even though Collin didn't crave blood as bad as the others, he doubted he could resist Lucifer's charm. There were very few who could, and most of them were Buddhist monks or other meditative men of that sort. Many Christian priests thought Lucifer tried harder with them because they taught God's word. That wasn't true—he tried the same with everyone. They were just weaker than they wanted to admit.

James found Gwen in the middle of an alley, sitting in the dirty, blood-tainted snow. She didn't even look up at him as he walked up to her.

He kicked her boot. "You left without saying a word."

She shook her head. "Not now, James. I really don't need any more shade."

"You should have thought about that before you ran

off by yourself without your phone."

She shook her head. "You could sense where I was."

"Yeah, but I didn't know if it was a trap. I wasn't going to risk everything, not to mention my skin, to come get you."

"Yes, you would have."

He let out a laugh. It was true. He was about to come get her when Lucifer showed up. Then he had to go report to him. "Do you need help up?"

"Probably. I haven't really tried. Didn't seem to be a point."

James knelt down and helped her stand. Her body felt limp, and he knew she wasn't doing it on purpose.

"So, what's going to be your excuse this time?" James asked as he helped her back to the hotel room.

She bit her lip as she glanced around. "First let's get back to the hotel. Then I'll explain."

"You just want more time to come up with a convincing lie."

She let out a brief chuckle. "Perhaps. Or perhaps I'm not sure myself. Actually, that's a lie. I know exactly what I was doing. However, I can't sense where they are and want to be extra safe."

"Well, it sounds like you have a plan that will outdo

all plans you have ever come up with."

"Damn straight. I endured a lot in the past twenty minutes. I had to make it pretty damn convincing."

That made James curious. Was she telling the truth? Did she have some elaborate plan, or was she acting on her emotions and making excuses? There was only one way to tell—get back to their hotel and make her tell him the truth. A couple of hours with the effects of the bite would make her come clean.

No one stopped him as he helped her to their hotel. That was one of the things James liked about Russia— everyone minded their own business. Usually, at least.

James carried Gwen the rest of the way up to their room and laid her on the couch. He went into the bathroom to grab a cloth to clean the blood off her neck and turned the gas fireplace on. He helped her out of her coat and boots, then she collapsed back and covered her face with her arm.

He took a seat across from her. "So, are you going to talk?"

"Yeah, just give me a second."

"Trying to figure out your lies?"

She shot him a look. "No, just a little tired and pissed off."

"Oh really? I'm a little bit pissed off too."

Gwen took a deep breath and then let it out slowly. "Okay. So I sensed Collin and went to see him."

"That you did."

"I went to see if it was a setup."

"Of which you could have triggered the trap and died."

She shook her head. "You think I can't take down both Erik and Elizabeth?"

He shrugged.

She went on. "And it was a trap. He had a flare gun in his pocket. He didn't just want to talk—he wanted me dead."

"So you finally got your wake-up call is what you're saying."

She nodded. "Yes. That's exactly what I am saying. And he was about to set it off when I set a new plan into motion. A way to set up the Gargoyles so I can rip out their hearts for betraying me."

James wasn't sure how their trap would set such a plan in motion. "Which is?"

"I got Collin to believe I wanted to help—that I would go to Seth, get info on what we are doing next, and bring it to him. Then I would sacrifice myself to the

Gargoyles."

He laughed. "There's no way they would believe that. Why would they?"

She grinned her sly, devilish grin. "Because Collin can sense where you all are in the city. And I have the best plan."

CHAPTER THIRTY-TWO

Erik

Erik bit at his nails as he stood on the balcony and peered out on the Russian city. He didn't like being there. He didn't think it was a good idea to be somewhere the demons always won. They had terrorized this city again and again. Most of Eastern Europe, actually. It was their favorite spot in all the world. Erik held out his hand as snow danced onto it. Perhaps they loved these places because they liked the way blood stained the pure whiteness of it all. He wouldn't put it past them.

Sighing, he put his hand down and leaned on the railing. He wasn't sure what to do next. They should leave and hide, but that would only cause the demons to smoke them out. Following them was clearly not doing anything, however, so Erik wasn't sure what would be the right option. He just wanted this to be over, but he also knew he couldn't give up.

The balcony door opened, and he turned to find Elizabeth stepping outside. She gripped her wool coat tightly. "You know, it's sort of chilly outside. We could ponder inside too. Where there is a heater."

He chuckled. "You know the cold doesn't bother us, right?"

She shivered. "Speak for yourself. We still can feel in this world. It just doesn't hurt us. But it sure is cold out still."

"We've been in colder places. Has it really been that long?" Erik asked.

She sighed. "I suppose it has. I'm just glad it's not fully winter yet. We should be out of here before the real cold sets in."

"Yeah. Hopefully. But for all we know, it will be

somewhere even colder. Like Antarctica or something."

She stepped up next to him and leaned on the railing. "And what exactly would demons want with Antarctica?"

He shrugged. "Who knows? They never make sense."

She laughed. "That's for sure."

"So, what do you think happened?"

"I think that Collin was about to shoot off the flare when Lucifer showed up."

"But then how did he make it out alive?"

She shook her head. "I have no idea. Perhaps he was distracted? Perhaps Gwen made Lucifer leave him alone?"

He took in a deep breath, the cold air making his body feel alert. "If that's the case, do you think she was trying to help him and that was what took so long in the first place? That she was trying to convince him that she was still having regrets?"

"I don't believe it. After what happened in Berlin, I really doubt she would come around. That fight was not a very clean one. If she really wanted to help, she wouldn't have put up as much of a fight."

Erik knew she had a point. "I guess we'll have to wait until Collin wakes up to tell us what happened."

"I guess so. But I still don't trust her."

"I know. Neither do I. I am just... curious, I guess."

"Why she would want to repent after all this time?"

Erik nodded. "Yes. I want to know if she has always felt this way or if it was just something recent."

"Or if it was all a ruse."

He shook his head. "It wasn't a ruse. They would have won already if it weren't for her. So there had to be something."

"I'm surprised she is still alive."

"I think the only reason the other demons didn't kill her was because of the blood bond she has with James. He was able to convince them that he would take care of it."

"Well, it took him long enough to do that. If it weren't for you, he probably would have never gotten her."

"Yeah... I suppose he wouldn't have. He wasn't gentle either. She must have been good at hiding all that time."

"She's good at manipulation is what she is. She probably was having too much fun with this world and didn't want it to end. I could see her pulling a stunt just to do that."

Erik knew she had a point. Gwen relished in chaos. It was what made her the scariest of the bunch. On top of the extra power with the blood bond, she always seemed unstoppable. But he had watched her closely as she followed him through the world. It would be one impressive plan if she was able to hold back her hunger for so long.

The door slid open, and Collin stuck his head out of the hotel room. "What are you guys doing out here?"

"Just taking a breather until you woke up," Erik explained as he headed toward the door. "I presume you want to stay inside?"

He nodded. "Yeah, it's a bit chilly outside. The cold isn't my favorite thing."

Erik and Elizabeth stepped inside. Collin took a seat on the couch and leaned forward with his elbows on his knees. The two of them sat across from him.

"So, I think I might have either helped or royally screwed up," he began.

Erik understood that feeling all too well.

Collin went on. "Only Gwen showed up. I was about to use the flare when… I don't know, she seemed so sad. It was like when I knew her before—back when I didn't know all this existed."

Elizabeth started to shake her head. "Don't believe her. She's a liar. She's the best liar."

"But you didn't know her when I did. She seemed human; she seemed sad and wanting to end it all."

Elizabeth stood up and began pacing. "No, Collin, you don't understand! You don't know what it was like to deal with her for two thousand years. She murdered our friends—she comes up with rhymes and games of how she slaughtered our brothers and sisters. She will drag on their death for as long as she can. If it weren't for the fact that she likes to play with us, both Erik and I would be dead. All this would have been over centuries before. But no, she has to torture us for a bit first."

Collin peered down, not wanting to meet eyes with Elizabeth. "I understand you all had a different experience with her, but my experience still happened. She brought me back to life when James almost killed me. It doesn't seem like something someone with no feelings would do. But how she looked tonight… It was like the Gwen I knew."

Erik understood what Collin meant. Even after all the torture he had been through, he still wanted to trust her. There was something in her eyes—something that told him she regretted everything. No other demon showed such feeling. Why was she different? Or was she really that good at acting?

"But before we could really talk, Lucifer showed up. He threatened Gwen a bit for everything she had done and then turned his attention to me. He promised me power, and I couldn't resist him. I don't even care for power, but his voice…"

Erik glanced over at Elizabeth, who nodded. "We understand, Collin. He can convince many people to do whatever he wants. You wouldn't be the first and aren't going to be the last."

"He would have succeeded in whatever he was going to do to me if it weren't for Gwen. She shoved him and distracted him so I could run." He looked back up and turned to both Elizabeth and Erik, staring them straight in the eyes. "She wouldn't have done that unless she really meant it."

Erik knew he made a fair point. She wouldn't be able to disobey him unless her will was strong, but that did lead to one possibility. "But if Lucifer stayed behind to deal with her, he will probably knock some sense into her, reminding her what is in store for her if she messes up."

Collin nodded. "I know. I know. That is why I am proposing the same plan, only a little different. Gwen promised me she wanted to kill herself. I think we should draw her out by letting her sense me, and if she comes alone with information and proof she is surrendering, then I'll signal to you to come finish her. If I sense any of the others, then we leave her."

It wasn't a bad plan, Erik had to admit. He couldn't see where it could go wrong, other than Collin endangering himself again. He had already done that, and Gwen hadn't killed him. He turned to Elizabeth. She was better at strategy than him.

She stood there, her arms crossed, pursing her lips. "I don't know. It sounds too good to be true. I don't trust it."

"But if we got her away from everyone, could it really go wrong?" Collin asked.

Elizabeth contemplated that. "I don't see how, but she has surprised me before. But you're right. You can sense them. You would know if something was up."

Collin nodded. "Exactly. You haven't had me on your side before. I think together, we can take her out, and then you would only have James and the others to deal with. It would be even, and I won't have to deal with this hunger any longer."

Erik felt bad for Collin. He had caused this human to suffer—it was his doing. But, he realized, it wasn't. It was Gwen and James and their ridiculous relationship. It was James's jealousy that had caused it, not Erik's fault. He was doing what God willed—even the Archangel Michael had said it was the right choice.

Erik got up. "I think it's a reasonable plan. I don't see where it could get us hurt. You can sense if they are coming, and we can run. It is safe and worth the low risk."

Elizabeth agreed. "You are right. When should we do this?"

"Tomorrow night," Collin said. "Or tonight since I suppose it's morning already. Sooner would be better, before Gwen has second thoughts."

CHAPTER THIRTY-THREE

Gwen

Gwen felt better after she'd had some of James's blood —at least good enough to go report to Seth and Jürgen about what had happened and what she'd set into motion. She headed up toward the meeting room that Seth had arranged. She bit at her lip, not looking forward to having to explain herself to them. They wouldn't have approved such tactics, but she had to. It was the only way to take down Elizabeth.

James pushed the button for the floor, and the elevator closed. "Oh, by the way, Jürgen revealed some information about you."

Great. More drama. "Oh? And what's that?"

"How you killed his wife."

She rolled her eyes. "Is he still upset about that? It happened centuries ago."

James watched her. Normally that was something he would agree with. Instead, he had a concerned look on his face. "Why didn't you tell me?"

Gwen pinched the bridge of her nose. "James, this isn't the time—"

"Well, since he just told us, I think you're going to have to make time. When I left, he was fuming."

Gwen let out a breath. "I don't know. It was so long ago. I guess I just... I didn't like the idea of Jürgen running off with some human. She wasn't one of us, and he was going to try to make her a hybrid."

"You know that's very two-faced, right?"

"I know, James. I know. But she was already crazy. She was a murderer and bathed in the blood of dozens upon dozens of young girls. She was more sadistic than I was, and that's saying something. Like, really sadistic."

"That wasn't your call. You should have told all of us if you had known. Then we could have discussed it."

Gwen shrugged. "Doesn't matter now. What happened has happened. End of story. When we open the gates of hell, he can ask Lucifer for her back. He knows that, but it's just that he has had to wait all this time."

James pursed his lips. He knew Gwen was right.

She yawned as she wrapped her arms around his neck. "I'm pretty tired from the bite. Can I have another snack?"

He still appeared a bit frustrated with her, but he moved his collar away from his neck. She bit him, his warm blood filling her mouth. It tasted sweet—like nothing else. It was like honey mixed with jasmine and citrus. It was everything she loved—he was everything she loved and she wouldn't let anyone take him away from her.

Gwen backed away and then kissed him on the lips. He licked the blood off his own lips and grinned. She gave him another peck, happy that she finally got him to lighten up. She already had to deal with everyone being pissed that she skipped out of the meeting with Lucifer to maybe trigger a trap. Well, there was a trap, but luckily she'd convinced Collin to believe her. Now she had a plan to take down at least one Gargoyle, if not both.

The elevator door opened, and they made their way to the meeting room. Seth and Jürgen glared at her as she took a seat and leaned back, placing her boots on the table. She wore a smirk that she could tell the other two didn't appreciate it. That made her even happier.

"Please tell me Lucifer got a good bite in or at least a slap or two. And that he killed that hybrid." Jürgen growled.

Gwen played at her nails. "A bite, a slap, but he didn't get the hybrid."

Jürgen slammed his fist on the table but didn't say anything.

Before anyone else could talk, Seth started to interrogate her. "Why did you leave without permission?"

She shrugged. "I sensed Collin, so I decided to check it out."

"So you jeopardized the mission again."

"No, I set it up so we can take one of them down."

Seth shook his head. "No, you screwed up and realized it, so you found a way to make it beneficial for you. That way we might not punish you."

"Perhaps. But either way, Collin believes I'll surrender myself after getting information from you all and then go to him alone so that the Gargoyles may do me in."

Seth shot out a laugh. "Seriously? You expect me to believe that?"

"I expect you to believe that I was able to use the emotions of a human who knew me as a caring individual. He was supposed to set off a flare gun for the Gargoyles to attack me but instead believed my lies. Then, to really seal the deal, Lucifer showed up. He threatened the hybrid, but I distracted him and Collin got away."

"You…" Seth took a deep breath. "Disobeyed Lucifer."

"So to speak. But in the end, it was for him, but it has made Collin think I'll actually help him." She grinned ear to ear.

Jürgen smacked the table. "Just get out with it. What do you plan to do? If you think you can take down the Gargoyles by yourself, you're greatly mistaken. They have Collin and can smell if the rest of us are nearby. What do you think you're going to do?"

"We are going to trick Collin. He isn't as… advanced as we are. So, if we can set up buckets of blood for James and Jürgen and you, Seth, we can make him believe that you all are still back here and they will think it's safe."

All three of them just stared at her. James opened his mouth and closed it again.

Seth leaned forward. "And then what? He will still smell us coming near."

"Which is why you all will be covered in my blood. It will mask your scent and make him believe it's just me in the meeting spot."

Seth started tapping his finger on the table, as if thinking about it.

Jürgen wrinkled his nose. "That's disgusting."

She turned to him. "But it will work. Theoretically. Probably. I'm pretty sure it will work."

"Well, that sounds promising." Set tapped his fingers some more. "But it does sound like a plan that could possibly work."

"See, I told you I had it covered."

"I'm not finished." Seth looked her straight in the eyes. "But if it goes wrong, I'll personally kill you. You understand that, right? They will try to kill you, but I'll step in and finish the job myself."

She sighed. "Don't worry, Seth. I won't fail."

Jürgen asked, "How do we know you're not tricking us? How do we know you aren't going to just snap and kill us all?"

Gwen reached in her coat pocket and pulled out the triduanum. "I'll stab myself with this to appear weak. Then you all attack, I get blood from James, and we slaughter them with their own knife. Oh, what fun it will be." She wiggled in her chair, excited.

James rubbed his temples. "So you're going to completely deplete yourself and think that you will be fine? That you will be safe during all this?"

"I already said I'll drink your blood. Besides, between the four of us, even if I was a little weak, I would be fine. We can take them out. All we need to do is target one of them, and I have a feeling the other will run away. I say we target the bitch Elizabeth since she was the one who murdered Darrell. Erik will have no choice but to leave her behind in order to salvage any chance he has in surviving."

Seth stood up and started pacing. "And what about your hybrid?"

She shrugged. "I have a feeling Erik will drag him

away with him for safekeeping, but if he stays to try to save Elizabeth, then Jürgen can have the satisfaction of killing him."

Jürgen grinned. "I like that plan."

She blew him a kiss. "You're welcome. Now, what do you all say? Is this a plan we are willing to risk?"

Seth glanced between Jürgen and James. Of everything, James seemed the most displeased. Gwen couldn't blame him as she was the one with the highest risk, and in a way that involved him. She smiled at all of them, trying to persuade them that she was excited for this.

"I say do it," Jürgen commented. "Worst-case scenario, Gwen dies and that we'll be rid of us a hybrid and herself."

James shot him a look but didn't argue.

"Fine," Seth said. "It's a plan. But you're going to have to feed tremendously beforehand to withstand losing all the blood you're proposing to use."

Her eyes flashed yellow. "Oh, I plan on getting my fill. Don't you worry."

"When do you think Collin will show himself again for us to do this?" Jürgen asked.

Gwen bit her lip. "Well, if I were him, I would be a

little freaked out meeting Lucifer, and then I would have to convince the Gargoyles of trying a plan, for which I myself compromised, again. He wouldn't want me to change my mind and would believe me weak because of Lucifer. I'd say tomorrow night. He might not show himself, but we could go ahead and try it on the outskirts of town. He will see that I am alone, which of course I won't be. Then he might be the decoy, so to speak, and I'll then stab myself with the triduanum, which will draw the Gargoyles out. Then you all grab Elizabeth, and I'll drink Collin's or James's blood to replenish myself."

Seth nodded. "That sounds like a plan. Go feed now, replenish yourself all day tomorrow, and we'll meet tomorrow evening before sundown here."

She grinned. "Looking forward to it."

CHAPTER THIRTY-FOUR

James

James wasn't sure if he liked the plan. Gwen was risking a lot—which included himself in the risk since they were connected. Also, even though he knew she hadn't been lying, he couldn't help but worry she really did want to help the Gargoyles. But if all went according to plan, they could take down a Gargoyle, tricking them just like they had in Berlin.

To be honest, he wanted to see their faces as they

realized Gwen's betrayal, or at least her trick. He doubted they believed her at all. If they were smart, they wouldn't. But Collin would, since he was a stupid human being, and because he loved her, he would try to convince them otherwise. He could sense where the rest of the demons were, which made him a threat. But the way Gwen was going to trick him, he wasn't convinced it was going to work. Would Collin really be fooled with a bucket of their blood and covering themselves with Gwen's own?

James had to admit, being covered in Gwen's blood was one of his favorite things, but he didn't like that Jürgen and Seth would be too. He supposed it wouldn't be too bad, but it would be a lot of blood on her part, on top of stabbing herself with the Triduanum. She would be weak, and he feared once the Gargoyles figured out what she did to set them up, they would kill her.

Which was why James would go straight to her, Jürgen and Seth would trap Elizabeth, and then the torturing would begin. That made James grin. If it was successful, it was going to be well worth it.

Gwen skipped in front of him as they went around Moscow, getting their fill. Although they had massacred the entire town in Poland, it had been a while since

James had gone on a killing spree like that. They weren't just making minions but actually feeding and killing. If it weren't for the fact that everything seemed to be recorded, they would have caused more chaos, but they didn't want to do that in case Collin or the Gargoyles were paying attention.

"Well, where to next?" Gwen asked as she twirled in the gentle falling snow. "A bar? A business? The docks?"

James considered that. "Zaryadye isn't as unpopular as it used to be. A lot of people visit there now. I don't think we can get away with anything. Not easily anyway."

She sighed. "Shady bar it is."

He laughed as he gave her a kiss on the cheek. Gwen took his hand and held it as they made their way down the street. He missed days like this where they could be together and do whatever they wanted—causing chaos. He missed the old days when there wasn't as big of a threat. In the beginning, when all the Gargoyles were still around, they did whatever they wanted without a plan, but after the deaths of comrades and the fact that only two Gargoyles were left, they had to be a bit more serious.

They found a small bar with a few people. Gwen didn't even wait but locked the door behind them and attacked the closest person she could. She bit him, blood spraying all across the table and chairs. James grabbed the bartender and bit him in the throat. Blood filled his mouth, and he drank way past his fill. He had been drinking all day. None of them were as delicious as Gwen's blood, but blood of a human was still satisfying. The screaming only added to it, like icing on a cake.

There had only been a handful of people, but they would be enough to finally finish their task of filling Gwen's power. The only blood that would give her any power would be his own. She would need that after she stabbed herself.

Blood covered all the tables and chairs after they were through. Gwen licked the blood off her fingers as she stepped over the last body of a middle-aged woman on the ground.

"Did you have your fun?" James raised an eyebrow.

"Of course. Now for the fun part of this mission."

"Buckets and buckets of your blood covering my skin?"

She grinned. "I figured you would think that was the

best part of it all."

He laughed. "Yes, well, I wish it was just me. But nevertheless, I am curious if it will work."

"It will work. Or at least I think it will."

"See, you don't even know."

"Well, we'll never know what works or doesn't work until it's over, will we?"

"I suppose. Well, should go meet up with the others?"

She nodded. "Yeah, let's get this going."

As she stepped outside and barred the door so no one could enter for a while, Gwen sniffed the air.

"Sense Collin yet?"

She shook her head. "No, not yet. But I know him—it will be tonight."

"You better be right or all that was wasted blood."

"I would never willingly waste blood. Don't worry, James."

He chuckled as they made their way through the city toward the business district. They entered the elevator and made their way up to where Jürgen and Seth were. The two of them also fed well as they had to fill buckets of their blood. But the scent was growing stronger. James knew they had already started.

The thought of filling a bucket with his own blood

felt a bit odd. It wasn't something they normally did nor had they ever had to. Usually the buckets were filled with human blood, if anything. But this plan—it was a long shot. If it worked, however, then they would win the war.

The elevator door opened, and they stepped onto the floor. Minions were busy at work with whatever Seth had planned. He didn't know the details, nor did he care. He hated all the paperwork and dealing with minions. If he had his way, everyone would be doing it themselves. Playing with chess pieces made the games even worse.

Just as expected, Jürgen and Seth were preparing the buckets. There were two spare ones for James to fill and Gwen to use to pour her blood to cover them.

Jürgen eyed them. "About time you showed up. I was beginning to think you had backed out."

Gwen sliced her wrist open and began filling a bucket. "We are here, aren't we? Besides, I don't sense him yet."

"And what if he doesn't? Then we wasted all this blood," Seth commented.

"We can put it in the fridge."

James rolled his eyes at her as he began to fill his

own bucket. "I'm still not sure this is going to work."

"I think it will," Gwen said. "There is no reason it wouldn't. If he can smell us because of our blood, my scent should drown you all out, and he should be able to smell all your blood here. We can leave a window open as well just to be safe. The Gargoyles can't sense anything, so we know that will be fine."

"Can I be the one to stab you with the triduanum?" Jürgen asked.

She grinned at him. "Unfortunately no. I must be the one to do that. Otherwise, it won't be convincing. I have to show them I'm willing to hurt myself. Speaking of which, Seth, did you get me some files I could act like I'm giving them?"

He nodded and threw a set of files on the table. "Here are some fake ones that we are going to go after Scandinavia next. We, of course, have already taken over those countries. If one of them gets away, they might think the details are real and go there only to find it a ruse. And we'll have gone through Asia by the time they figure it out."

Gwen smiled as she finished filling the bucket. James licked her wrist as he healed the wound. She did the same to his after he finished his bucket. Seth and Jürgen looked at them with disgust. Gwen stuck her tongue out at them as she held up her bucket. "So, who's ready to be covered in my blood?"

James held up his hand. Neither of the other two appeared excited for the endeavor. James began to take his tie and shirt off. Jürgen raised an eyebrow.

"What are you doing?"

James shrugged. "Wouldn't it be easier if we covered our bodies under our clothes? Not sure if you noticed, but it's a bit chilly outside. I don't want my clothes to be that wet."

"This mission keeps getting worse and worse by the minute."

Gwen grabbed a ladle and began pouring blood all over James after he stripped down to his trunks. It took all his willpower not to lick the blood off himself. It smelled divine—like honey and everything sweet.

Moving to the others, Gwen poured blood onto them. Neither Jürgen nor Seth seemed amused or excited for it. If anything, they appeared defeated. But James knew it was worth the risk, and they would be able to take Elizabeth down.

Gwen took a deep breath and grinned. "Right on time. I smell Collin now. He's on the complete edge of town just like last time. Warehouse district, if I'm not mistaken. They probably made all the people leave the area and think they can trap me. This will work to our benefit."

James grabbed his clothes and started to put them back on. "And if they try to blow up the area?"

"Well, then shit. It didn't kill us the first time; it won't kill us this time. How about Jürgen and Seth stay a little away from the building, then when Collin signals, they can move in?"

"Seems fair. Worst-case scenario, I get to see Gwen go up in flames, and I don't disagree with that."

Gwen clapped her hands together. "Well then, shall we?"

CHAPTER
THIRTY-FIVE

Collin

Collin paced back and forth on the warehouse floor, waiting for Gwen. He could sense her coming. It was a bit stronger than normal. Perhaps he was hungry and his senses were hyperaware of her, as that was what they were craving. He felt as if he had gone weeks without water or food and needed her more than anything. If for some reason he didn't die tonight, he wasn't sure what he was going to do. He couldn't go on like this—he needed either her blood or a human's to keep going. Perhaps Gwen would give him her blood. He prayed that was the case.

According to his senses, the others were still in the business district. They seemed weaker, but he was tired and felt hyperfocused on Gwen. Perhaps Gwen knocked them out so she could escape without them knowing. That seemed logical, knowing her.

This time he wasn't using a flare, but Erik and Elizabeth were nearby, watching from the rafters above. Gwen wouldn't expect them so close, and they wanted to witness what she was going to do. He couldn't blame them, as he wouldn't expect her to turn herself in. Not many would sacrifice themselves in such a way.

Collin realized that was exactly what he was doing, however, as he was waiting for his own death. Gwen might kill him, or if the Gargoyles were able to kill her, then he would die with her. But he was ready to stop this agony—he doubted he could stand it much longer. The thirst was too much.

She was getting closer. Collin wondered how she was traveling—if she was using her superspeed or taking a cab. The cabs were a bit terrifying in Moscow, but he knew she didn't have anything to worry about. If the driver was some creep, she would just kill him. She was way more of a threat than most humans could be. As for scarier, he wasn't quite sure.

Gwen was close now. Collin felt his heart race as he paced in the warehouse. He wasn't quite sure what this warehouse held as everything was in giant crates. Was it stuffed animals? Was it cookware? The Holy Grail? He didn't know and didn't care to find out. The Gargoyles had made everyone leave so that if a fight broke out, it wouldn't harm anyone. The cameras were also turned off.

Collin gulped as he sensed her nearby. Her scent was strong—almost intoxicating. He took deep breaths trying to calm himself down and trying not to turn into the monster he had always been fighting inside.

He couldn't be that monster—he was not a demon. He was not an animal. He was a human, and nothing would change that.

After a bit, he was able to relax. Her scent almost seemed to surround him, but she was stepping inside the warehouse. He felt her as she zigzagged through the boxes, searching for him. As she rounded a corner, Collin saw her. She fidgeted with her coat, almost appearing as if she were crying.

They stared at each other for a moment, not saying a word. Collin wasn't sure what to say, as they both knew what was coming. He finally found the words. "Thank you, for yesterday I mean. For saving me."

She shook her head. "I couldn't let him take you like that. You shouldn't have to suffer like I've had to all these years."

He felt bad that she'd had to deal with someone like that. It made sense why she couldn't run. It also showed him how much courage she had to try to disobey a creature like that. He wasn't sure in her position if he could have done the same thing.

Gwen reached into her coat. "I have the information on the next attack strategy. It seems that Seth wants to attack the Nordic nations as they have a lot of resources for the taking. Another cold country, am I right?" She smiled, but it was an empty smile.

Collin took the files and flipped through them. They appeared authentic, but he didn't have any way of knowing. The Gargoyles would be able to tell, however. "Thank you. I didn't think you would have been able to acquire anything like this."

She shrugged. "I distracted them. It's easy when James trusts me."

"Will you miss him?" Collin asked. It was a stupid question and not a question he should have asked.

"Well, I doubt I'll be away from him that long since I know Lucifer has a special little place for us in hell together. And I'm sure he will remind me each and every day how much I hurt him." She appeared as if she wanted to cry again.

Collin wasn't sure if he should step up and comfort her or if he should let her be. It wasn't exactly an easy decision for a lover who was an ex and wasn't sure if he really meant anything to a demon who was connected to another demon through a blood bond. It was hard enough when it was just exes who had mutual friends, so they didn't try to make a scene for them.

"What made you change your mind?" Collin asked. "I mean, I know what happened decades ago, but what about now? It was clear that James had made you snap. I was there. Then after what the Gargoyles did… I didn't expect this."

She shrugged, tears filling her eyes. "I just… I just can't do this anymore. I have seen so much destruction, so much chaos. I just want it all to stop. Lucifer isn't going to win. He told us a long time ago if we were able to kill the Son of God, we would be free, and that wasn't true. Then after he was resurrected again, he said we could open the gates of hell." She shook her head. "I have my doubts. I think even if we kill the Gargoyles that there will just be another thing come up and all those promises will go out the window. I want it to be over. I want this fighting to be over."

Collin could understand what she was saying. He had been caught in family drama where people promise something, and after he did everything he could to help that person, they simply blew him off. On such a grand scale, he would have wanted it all to end too. He wanted it to end when he was at home, which was why he ran away to London.

"What do you want to do, Gwen?" Collin asked. "The Gargoyles won't let you near them. They don't trust you."

She laughed. "I don't blame them. I have done countless things to all of them. I deserve whatever punishment Lucifer has in store for me from what I did to them alone. Then all the humans I have killed, all the torturing and pain I have caused… It's a miracle God Himself hasn't shot down lightning to destroy me on the spot. But I suppose He can't since He isn't a part of this fight. If he intervened, all us demons would be dead."

If they posed such a threat, why wouldn't He just destroy them? It didn't make sense to Collin, but a lot about their world didn't make sense to a human like him.

"I...," Collin began, not sure of the words. "I can't bring myself to hurt you. But if you're really willing to turn yourself in, raise your hands so the Gargoyles can finish the job."

Gwen smiled a little as she reached in her pocket. Collins stepped back, not sure what she would need to grab, when she pulled out something he did not expect. It was the triduanum—the blade that had pierced Jesus's side.

Before he could realize what she was going to do with it, Gwen stabbed herself in the stomach.

CHAPTER THIRTY-SIX

Erik

Erik couldn't believe his eyes. Gwen just stabbed herself in the stomach with the triduanum.

He stared down at Collin and Gwen as she went down on her knees and let out a scream. He couldn't imagine stabbing himself in the stomach like that. It had to hurt, and not only that, she was now weakened tremendously by its effects.

Glancing over at Elizabeth, they both nodded. This

was it—Gwen was really sacrificing herself to bring down the demons. He didn't question it—there wasn't time to question it. She was weak. Collin could sense the others were far away. This couldn't go wrong.

But that was far from the truth.

The moment they jumped down from the rafters, he saw them appear like shadows. Jürgen and Seth, covered in blood, heading straight for Elizabeth. This had been a trap.

Erik needed to decide. Was he going to help Elizabeth, or was he going to take Gwen out while she was weak? She went this far to convince them that she was going to help just to draw them out. It was a risk, and she would be hoping that he would help Elizabeth. Erik leaped straight toward Gwen, but he wasn't fast enough. A figure grabbed her and took her back away from Erik. He hit the ground, mumbling a few words under his breath as he watched Gwen bite the neck of James, who was also covered in blood.

She had planned this carefully. She must have had some sort of decoy scent, probably the other three's blood, in the place that they were usually at, then masked their scent from Collin by covering them in her blood. Then to seal the deal for him and Elizabeth to show up was to stab herself. She knew they would jump down, and James was there—waiting.

Erik had to admit, this was well played. He glanced over to Collin, who stood there, confused, with his mouth open. Erik knew he needed to grab him and run. He peered back at Elizabeth who now was caught by the two demons. They held her down on the ground.

"Erik! Run!" Elizabeth screamed. "You have to get out of here! It was a trap!"

He didn't want to leave without her, however, as he knew there would be no way for him to win this war alone. But she was right—there was no way he could get her out of this without risking his own skin. Which meant he needed to focus on Collin first.

Turning back to Collin, he went forward to grab him, but Gwen used her superspeed to grab him first.

She laughed. "Not so fast. He has to witness what I am about to do to her. He has to know what trusting me has cost you all."

Erik shook his head. "You are a monster. You know he trusted you because he believed in you. And now you're going to torture him like that?"

"Of course. I'm a demon after all. He needs to learn that for creatures like me, there is no redemption.

There's no honor in war; there is no reason to repent. I am darkness, chaos, and evil. I can't be anything else. Our God has forbidden that, hasn't He?"

He looked back at Elizabeth as the demons covered in blood pinned her down.

She glared at him. "Run, you idiot!"

Erik didn't know what to do. He didn't want to leave, losing both his colleagues. But it looked as if he didn't have a choice. Collin still appeared to be in shock and didn't try to fight back as Gwen pulled him close like a teddy bear. Her eyes flashed yellow as she bared her teeth to Erik. James stepped up next to her as he watched Erik, as if stalking his prey.

He needed to get out of there. He didn't have any other choice.

Erik leaped up, using his wings to fly out of there.

"Run, little Gargoyle! It is what you're best at!" Gwen laughed.

He held back the tears as he soared through the building and out the back. None of the demons stopped him—they knew that if they didn't focus on one, then it was possible for Elizabeth to get away. He put some distance between them and the warehouse and collapsed. He pounded his fist on the cold, snowy ground.

"No," he whispered. "It can't end like this. I can't let them take them."

Erik knew he had to figure out something. He had to find a way to save Elizabeth and Collin. He took a few deep breaths. Elizabeth would be harder, so the main priority was Collin as he could locate the demons. At least with him, Erik knew they could stay hidden and come up with a plan. If Erik was alone, he would be going at this blind.

Elizabeth was the smart one though. She was the one who needed to survive. Erik thought about going in and asking for a trade—his life for hers. But he knew they would just double-cross him. He had nothing to give but everything to lose.

He realized they couldn't sense him. He still had on the Holy water. He could sneak in as their focus would be on Elizabeth. He cringed at the scene he knew he would find. Would Gwen string her up? Would she slowly chop her up into pieces? It was a scene he did not want to see.

Pondering on whether he wanted to call the cops, he decided not to. It would either end in him finding out they had already been turned into minions or they would be slaughtered and then turned into minions.

"Think, Erik, think!" He paced back and forth. He had never been this alone before. He didn't know what to do.

Going in was the only good idea. They wouldn't think he would be stupid enough, and then he could get an idea of how to grab Collin, and hopefully Elizabeth, and run. It was his only hope.

He snuck back toward the warehouse. So far he didn't see anyone. They hadn't brought minions since Collin could sense them. They must have fed all day to gather their strength, and they did it slowly so Collin wouldn't notice. They learned from Berlin.

Gwen must have really understood the risk, and the others probably only agreed because she was the one holding all the risk. He was surprised James would have gone along with it, but it was apparent that he was close by just in case. Erik wished they learned and knew better. They shouldn't have trusted Collin's assessment of Gwen. Though she was pretty convincing. Even Erik was beginning to believe her.

As he approached the warehouse, he searched around for any of the demons. They would need all four to keep Elizabeth pinned down, he knew, and to keep an eye on Collin. He slowly entered the warehouse and leaped back up into the rafters. From there, he could see the entire floor and where they were holding Elizabeth.

He hid back so he could see but he didn't stand out. They had Elizabeth chained up by her legs from one of the cranes in the room. Blood dripped from her mouth and nose, down her forehead and onto the ground. Collin was tied to a chair with metal chains as well. Erik didn't think he was really trying to get away but still in shock for what Gwen had done. She had completely shattered him now.

Gwen was standing between Collin and Elizabeth, grinning with satisfaction. Erik wasn't sure if it was satisfaction in capturing Elizabeth or for what she had done to Collin. She pulled out the triduanum and pointed it at Elizabeth.

"Let's see if we can have a little fun, shall we?"

CHAPTER THIRTY-SEVEN

Gwen

Gwen wanted to take as much time as possible in dealing with Elizabeth, but she had a feeling Erik would try anything to rescue her or Collin. She knew as well as him that there would be no way he could save both. He wouldn't be able to take all the demons out and grab two injured colleagues. No, he had to choose, and he was planning this wisely.

She had a feeling it would be Collin. It would be the

wisest choice, as otherwise Erik would be trying to fight blind like the Gargoyles had been all this time. They couldn't sense where they were, but Collin could. He would be more aware of what was going on versus one blind mouse against a bunch of feral cats.

Gwen turned her attention back to Elizabeth. She had been waiting for this day for so long. Elizabeth was one of the Gargoyles that had caused her the most trouble over the years. Never would she have imagined that she would get to do the honors. She would be able to get revenge for Darrell, make Collin crack, and be one step closer to fulfilling Lucifer's wish.

Gwen knelt down so that her face was level with Elizabeth, who was hanging upside down from the chains that they had tied her up with. She smiled at her. "I can't believe you fell for our trap. You have no idea how happy this makes me."

"You fell for my trap earlier. I guess we are even then."

Gwen could hear the fear in Elizabeth's voice. That made her smile even larger. She studied her face, trying to make sure she remembered the agony and blood that dripped down her mouth and nose into her hairline. Gwen wiped away a little of it with her finger and licked it. Although James's blood was the best in every aspect of the word, something about drinking the blood of a Gargoyle was intoxicating. Was it because it wasn't defiled like theirs had been? Was it because it was something pure that had been taken away from them? She wished she could bathe in it all, and perhaps she would.

She stood back up. "Well, first thing's first, of course. We have to take away your ability to fly. Those pesky wings always seem to be our downfall, don't they, boys?"

All three of the demons laughed. Gwen took a peek at Collin to find his face still shocked and horrified. He hadn't said much, which surprised Gwen. Perhaps he knew this was the end and simply accepted it—just like he should.

"Real classic, Gwen. Take away the thing that you're so jealous of."

Gwen pulled out the triduanum. "Jealous? Perhaps. But at least I am free and don't have to follow all the laws that you do."

Elizabeth spat out blood. "Ha. Free. Good one. Do you really think yourself free? How long has it been, Gwen? That all you demons have been stuck in this world, obeying the whims of Lucifer? Centuries upon centuries? And when you thought you were finally free, you have another impossible task to complete. Two thousand years later and you still haven't accomplished it."

Gwen laughed. "Impossible task? I don't think you realize, but you're about to die. And we'll only have Erik to destroy. There is no way he is going to be able to take us all on. We can make countless minions. Face it, you lost your chance to take us down in Berlin. That was your one shot, and you blew it."

"You all got lucky. If all five of you had been there, you would all be dead."

"You are probably right, but clearly your God doesn't care if you win or lose; otherwise, he would have made sure it went without a hitch." Gwen traced her back. "Now, where are those pesky wings of yours? Oh right, exactly where my scars are."

Using the triduanum, she found the bottom of where the wings met his back and began to slice the skin where she knew they connected. Elizabeth let out a high-pitched scream.

"Stop it!" Collin finally had the mindset to speak. "If you're going to kill her, just kill her. You don't need to torture her like this!"

Gwen turned to him. "I think I do. It's been centuries of them pestering us. This is just the way we say goodbye, right Jürgen?"

Jürgen grunted. "Yup."

Collin glared at her, shaking his head. "This isn't you. You are putting up a front for the other demons. You want to be seen as a monster so they don't realize you doubt everything."

Gwen laughed as she kept on cutting up Elizabeth's back. Elizabeth tried her best to bite her tongue but couldn't help but scream. "Oh, Collin. You don't know me. The time we have been together, the time you have been alive, is just like a blink of an eye to us. We have lived for an eternity. Time means nothing to us, and little mistakes I have made while with you are just that. Boredom of all the time I have been alive."

Seth rolled his eyes. "Yes, other than you cost us almost everything with your little boredom."

She shot him a look. "But here we are, almost done, Seth. Tell you what, you can take off the next wing." She tossed him the triduanum. His eyes went wide as the blade was aiming straight for him. He caught it by the handle in the air.

"Hey! Be careful with that! You could have sliced me!"

"I am being generous."

"James, do something about her. She's getting playful, and nothing good ever comes of that."

James stepped up to her and wrapped his arms around her. "Oh, I disagree." He kissed her on the lips.

Gwen ran her hands through his blood-encrusted hair. Gwen turned back to Seth. "See, Seth? It's only you who gets upset. You just like causing drama."

He ignored her as he dug the knife into Elizabeth. "It's amazing, is it not? How much pain both Gargoyles and demons can withstand without passing out? Lucky for us you can't go anywhere."

Once he had carved the rest of her back, he handed the knife to Jürgen. Jürgen studied Elizabeth, not sure where to start. "Should I start at the fingers? The legs so she can't run? So many choices."

Elizabeth thrashed around as Jürgen stepped closer. That didn't do anything but cause her to sway back and forth from the crane that held her chained up.

"Jürgen Vlad, Seth Shezmu, Guinevere Erebus, and James Arthur. I'm not surprised it's you four that are left. However, I am surprised that you haven't gone and tried to kill one another," Elizabeth said.

Jürgen laughed. "Nice try. We know we hate each other. You aren't going to reveal any secrets that will make us turn on one another."

"No, but I can rehash old memories. Such as your wife Elizabeth Bathory. Weren't you going to turn her into a hybrid? And then Gwen killed her."

He grabbed her hand. "Yup." He sliced off her pinkie.

Elizabeth screamed. Gwen was thankful that they had already rehashed that a day ago. Otherwise, that tactic might have worked.

"It's why I'll stop at nothing to open the gates of hell. I want to bring her back. That is the promise Lucifer made me."

Elizabeth laughed. "You think Lucifer has that power? He doesn't have the power to bring back a human soul from the dead. He lies. You all know this. Why can't you get it through your thick skulls?"

"He may lie to humans," Gwen said as she folded her arms. "But he doesn't lie to us. Now, you're talking hasn't gotten you anywhere, so just shut up."

"You would like that, wouldn't you, Gwen? You are the one who has caused everyone problems over these years. I'm sure I could hit a nerve if I keep trying."

Gwen held out her hand. "Jürgen, the knife."

He handed it to her.

She nodded toward Elizabeth. "Now, who wants to hold her mouth open while I cut her tongue out?"

Collin started shouting. "No! Don't!"

Gwen ignored him as Seth held open Elizabeth's mouth. It had been quite a while since Gwen sliced someone's tongue off, and with such a large knife, she wasn't very clean about it. She ended up slicing Elizabeth's lips and jaw a bit along with her tongue. Blood came pouring down from her mouth and into her nose and across her face. She hacked and coughed as blood began to choke her.

"Are you crazy?" Collin shouted. "She's choking!"

Gwen turned to him. "Uh, that's the point? Don't worry, we have a lot more in store for her. We are just getting started. Fingers and arms and legs. Ears, nose, oh so much." She stepped up to him and bent down to his level. "Unless you want us to cut you up instead. Never have really physically tortured a hybrid. I wonder how much pain you can really take."

Collin glared at her. "No, you'd rather torture me by forcing me to watch. That is why you tied me up like this."

She grinned. "Well, yeah. But don't worry. After this is over, I promised Jürgen he could kill you."

"That you did," Jürgen agreed as he took the knife from Gwen's hand. "My turn to take off more fingers."

"Have at it. I'll stay here and keep Collin company." She knelt down and placed her arm around Collin so she could whisper in his ear. "Now watch very closely. See that beautiful red liquid? Doesn't it smell oh so intoxicating?"

"This is not amusing. This is disgusting."

"Then why are your eyes shining yellow? Admit it, you hunger for the blood that is spilling."

Collin shook his head. "Not like this."

"It's your instinct. Give in to it. Wouldn't it be amazing to go and drink her blood? Have the richness fill your mouth?"

"You know as well as I the only blood I can stomach is yours."

Gwen leaned in closer to his ear, almost touching him. "That is only because you're associating love with blood. Your humanity is what is stopping you from stomaching any other blood. If you just let it go, you could drink anyone's blood."

"No. I'll never let go of my humanity. It is the only

thing I have left."

Gwen sighed as she stood up. James, Jürgen, and Seth had sliced up Elizabeth pretty good now. She struggled and coughed, but it was to no avail. Her death was coming. Gwen glanced up to the rafters. It was Erik's move now. Who was it going to be? His colleague of two thousand years or the human that he made her turn?

CHAPTER THIRTY-EIGHT

Collin

Collin wanted to look away, but Gwen was right—he wanted that blood that spilled out of every cut that came off Elizabeth. It made him hungry and sick at the same time. He bent to the opposite side of Gwen and threw up what bile he had in his stomach. He hadn't eaten in a couple of days, so nothing was left.

He hadn't had blood for a long time either, which made matters worse. It was a painstaking thirst that gnawed at him every moment of every day. The smell of Gwen's blood covered the three demons. Now he understood why she smelled so strong to him when she came—it was because the others were covered in it. It was what he thirsted for more than the blood that was dripping off Elizabeth. It was within reach and yet so far.

Tugging on the chains, he knew it was no use. He was too weak. There was no way he could do anything. All he could do was sit there and take in the horror that hung before him. He just prayed Erik made it out and that he would take out these demons once and for all. It would be something he would want to see from Heaven.

She leaned over and whispered in his ear again. He wondered if she did it to make the hair on his skin stick up or so the others would hear her as they seemed preoccupied by torturing Elizabeth. "Say to me what you want, and perhaps I'll give it to you."

"Why would you do that? Don't you want me weak so I can't fight back?" Collin knew it had to be a lie. She was just playing with him. He needed to learn that was her true nature—there was no good left in her. The Gargoyles had been right. But he believed her, and now

Elizabeth was paying the cost.

"Perhaps. Or perhaps I want to hear the words and will follow through with my promise. Now say it. Say you want my blood."

Collin didn't want to admit it—he didn't want to admit the thirst and agony. He didn't want to admit that he thirsted for it every moment. "Fine. I want your blood."

She placed her wrist against his lips, and before he knew what was happening, he had already bitten her skin, and her blood was now filling his mouth and satisfying his thirst. He felt energy coming back to him. It was like drinking five energy drinks but not dealing with the heart attack that would cause. His heart was beating fast, yes, but it was steady and strong.

"Gwen! What are you doing!" James exclaimed.

She giggled. "I couldn't help it. He looked so thirsty."

Jürgen shook his head. "No, you're planning something! What is it?"

She shook her head. "Nothing." She stepped toward them. "I mean, what could I really possibly be planning. I already told you, Jürgen, you could have him once this was over. But did you really want something as weak and pathetic as he was? Or did you want something more interesting?"

Seth took out the knife he had stabbed Elizabeth with. "Damn it, Gwen, I swear to Lucifer if you fuck this up for us again—"

He didn't have time to finish that sentence when Collin felt something drop from the ceiling behind him. Suddenly the chair he found himself on was lifted up in the air. He glanced behind him to find Erik. He couldn't believe what he was seeing. Was Erik really saving him instead of Elizabeth?

Gwen shouted from the ground. "So that is your choice then, Erik? The hybrid instead of pretty little Elizabeth?" She stepped up to Elizabeth's hanging body. "Two little Gargoyles with nowhere to run, cut one up…" She stabbed her hand through Elizabeth's chest and pulled out her heart. In an instant, Elizabeth's body turned to dust. "And there was one!"

Erik didn't say anything as he flew the two of them out of the warehouse. Erik didn't stop for a while until he thought it was clear. Collin could understand that, but he needed to do something about his scent—he needed Holy water so that the demons couldn't follow them.

Once they did finally stop, which was outside of town and the opposite direction of the hotel, Erik broke him out of his chains and handed him a bottle of Holy water. As he covered himself, Erik collapsed to his knees and started weeping. Collin wasn't sure what to do but simply knelt down beside him and placed his hand on his back.

CHAPTER THIRTY-NINE

James

James glared at Gwen. "Damn it! You knew he was up there, and you let him take the hybrid!"

He didn't even stop Jürgen as Jürgen threw a punch at her. Instead of fighting back, she just laughed.

"But this will make it all the more fun! Come on, guys, lighten up! He's just a hybrid."

Seth picked up the triduanum and stabbed her with it. This time she let out a scream.

"You bitch! You know he can track us! If I see his face, he's dead, do you hear me? I'm not playing around anymore. And I'm not letting James heal you until the last moment for this knife wound! Maybe by then you will have learned your lesson!"

Gwen gasped and moaned. "But we got Elizabeth. She was the only one who posed a threat. We can still smoke Erik out. He's going to go hide in some church. He poses no risk. Come on, Seth! Lighten up!"

Seth kicked her in the side. "Then why didn't you just kill him? We can't blow this, Gwen, or we'll be tortured forever! Do you hear me?"

She nodded. James sighed. He liked having playful Gwen back, but things were too tense for how carefree she was. It was almost like…

No. She wouldn't be trying to self-destruct, knowing that she can neither have redemption nor make it seem she was trying to help the Gargoyles. She didn't have a conscious. Not after how she went about torturing Elizabeth. But James realized she gave Collin blood and stepped away, knowing she left him open enough for Erik to grab. He clenched his fist.

Why would she betray them like that again? No, he couldn't let her get away with this. He would keep a close eye on her—he would find out what was really going through her mind, and he would put an end to it. He had to.

Seth clapped his hands together. "Well, that is a wrap here. On to the next country? So we can smoke them out?"

Jürgen and James nodded. James bent down and grabbed Gwen to carry her. She wasn't going to be able to move for a couple of days with that wound. And he agreed. She needed to learn her lesson. And so did he.

CHAPTER FORTY

Erik

"Erik, what are we going to do?" Collin asked.

Erik didn't know. He paced in their room in the Vatican. Only one candle was lit now, and Erik didn't know what to do next. The entire church was praying for him—praying that God would save them all from the coming of Lucifer. Erik wasn't sure what he could do to stop them.

He turned to Collin. At least he had a way to find them, if they were within a certain range. He supposed really it was a matter of knowing when they had been found so they could run away. Was that what he was going to do for the next century? Two centuries? How much time was he going to waste? Should he just let them kill him? Should he just go find them and fight to the death? He didn't know.

"Erik…," Collin began to ask again.

"I don't know! All right? I. Don't. Know."

Collin's eyes went wide. Erik felt a bit bad for snapping at him. He sighed as he sat down next to him.

"I'm sorry. I just… We need some time to figure out what we are going to do next, okay? Give it some time."

Collin nodded. "All right. I guess we have all the time in the world, don't we?"

Erik glanced out of the window at the city. "Unfortunately."

Thank you so much for reading! Readers like you make it possible for authors like me to write stories! If you could spare a moment and leave a review on Amazon, Goodreads, BookBub, and wherever you like to buy books, that would mean the world to me! It really helps authors like me to succeed in the publishing world.

Book 3: The Redeemed coming June 2021!

Acknowledgements

This novel has been many years in the making and am so excited to finally get it out for readers to enjoy. There are many people who helped make this possible, including my mentors Mike, Joe, Betty, Paul, and many more over the years. I also want to give a big thank you to my editors Chantelle and Justin who have been encouraging me to keep writing since we first met, and to my new editor and friend Hilary who found interest in my story and wanted to be involved. I also want to say thank you to my writing group, Bernie, Traci, Rebecca, Stacy, and Christi who have been so helpful and great readers, editors, and listeners. To my friends, including Earlene, Veronica, Faye, Dave, and Amelia who helped edit and give feedback, thank you as well! Thank you Biserka Designs for the wonderful cover! To my parents who have helped through the years to keep on going. And lastly, to my husband who has stuck by my side, helping me through it all.

About the Author

Dani Hoots is a science fiction, fantasy, romance, and young adult author who loves anything with a story. She has a B.S. in Anthropology, a Masters of Urban and Environmental Planning, a Certificate in Novel Writing from Arizona State University, and a BS in Herbal Science from Bastyr University.

Currently she is working on a YA urban fantasy series called Daughter of Hades, a YA urban fantasy series called The Wonderland Chronicles, a historic fantasy vampire series called A World of Vampires, and a YA sci-fi series called Sanshlian Series. She has also started up an indie publishing company called FoxTales

Press. She also works with Anthill Studios in creating comics through Antik Comics.

Her hobbies include reading, watching anime, cooking, studying different languages, wire walking, hula hoop, and working with plants. She is also an herbalist and sells her concoctions on FoxCraft Apothecary. She lives in Phoenix with her husband and visits Seattle often. Feel free to email her with any questions you might have!

danihootsauthor@gmail.com